In 1995 Jack Higgins was awarded an honorary doctorate by L... Metropolitan University. He is a fellow of the Royal Society of Arts and an expert scuba diver and marksman. He lives on Jersey.

ALSO BY JACK HIGGINS

JACK HIGGINS

The Khufra Run

HARPER

Harper
An Imprint of HarperCollins*Publishers*
77–85 Fulham Palace Road,
Hammersmith, London W6 8JB

www.harpercollins.co.uk

This paperback edition 2009
1

First published in Great Britain by Macmillan & Co Ltd
under the name of James Graham in 1972.
Then by Grafton books in 1974

Copyright © James Graham 1972

Jack Higgins asserts the moral right to
be identified as the author of this work

A catalogue record for this book is
available from the British Library

ISBN: 978-0-723471-4

Typeset in Sabon by Palimpsest Book Production Limited,
Grangemouth, Stirlingshire

Printed and bound in Great Britain by
Clays Ltd, St Ives plc

Publisher's Note

THE KHUFRA RUN was first published in the UK by Macmillan & Co Ltd in 1972 and later by Grafton in 1974. It was originally published under the name of James Graham an author who later became known to millions as Jack Higgins.

This amazing novel has been out of print for some years, and in 2009, it seemed to the author and his publishers that it was a pity to leave such a good story languishing on his shelves. So we are delighted to be able to bring back THE KHUFRA RUN for the pleasure of the vast majority of us who never had a chance to read the earlier editions.

In memory of George Robert Limón

Contents

1
Night Flight

It was late evening when they brought the coffin down to the lower quay in Cartagena's outer harbour. There were no family mourners as far as I could see, just four men from the undertakers in the hearse, a customs officer in a Land-Rover bringing up the rear.

One useful extra that comes with an Otter Amphibian is the fact that you can drop wheels beneath the floats and taxi out of the water on to dry land if it suits your purpose. This was exactly what I'd done now, running up on to the concrete slipway at the bottom of the steps which would certainly make loading the coffin easier.

Two or three seamen leaned against the

sea wall watching, attracted by the novelty of the floatplane as much as anything else, an exotic enough item to find down there among the fishing boats and yachts.

The hearse braked to a halt, three of the men inside got out and went round to the rear to deal with the coffin. The fourth moved to join me.

Undertakers are the same the world over and Jiminez was no exception, a tall, cadaverous creature in a double-breasted black overcoat who seemed to exist in a permanent state of mourning. He raised his Homburg briefly and held out two fingers for the good and sufficient reason that this was all he had left on his right hand. 'Ah, Senor Nelson, we meet again. A melancholy business.'

He produced a small silver box, inhaled a pinch of snuff vigorously then shook his head, an expression of settled gloom on his face so that one might have been excused for imagining the deceased to have been a very old and dear friend.

'I know,' I said, 'but the rest of us just have to keep on going somehow.'

'True,' he said, 'very true,' and he took a sheaf of documents from his inside breast pocket as the customs officer got out of his Land-Rover and joined us.

'Senor Nelson.' He held out his hand with the usual Spanish courtesy. 'At your orders.'

'At yours, Senor,' I replied.

'And how is Ibiza these days?'

'Fine,' I said, 'or otherwise, depending on how the charters go.'

He examined the papers briefly. 'Juan Pasco, aged eighteen. So young?'

He glanced at Jiminez who shrugged. 'Killed in a car crash. A university student. You know how it is. The parents wish him to be laid to rest in the family vault back home in Ibiza.'

'Naturally.' The customs man nodded. The other three men shuffled by with the coffin on a trestle and he held out a hand to arrest them. 'Gentlemen, it pains me to have to ask, but I must look inside, simply to see that all is as it should be. I have my orders, you understand?'

It was a ritual we had gone through on

the four previous occasions I'd been engaged in the same line of work, and to be expected. Coffins had, after all, been known to contain other things than bodies and with Ibiza a part of metropolitan Spain, the flight from Cartagena counted as an internal one with no customs inspection at the other end.

'But of course, Senor,' Jiminez told him gravely. 'You must do your duty.'

He waved a hand, the coffin was set down, the gilt handles unscrewed quickly, the lid removed.

Some people appear to shrink in death. Certainly the boy in the coffin seemed no more than thirteen, although the face had been so heavily made up with cosmetics that he resembled a waxworks dummy. Nothing human about him at all. I presumed that most of the damage was covered by the stiff blue suit.

Jiminez took another pinch of snuff. 'The skull was crushed and the flesh completely removed from the left cheek by the impact. One would never guess now, of course.'

The customs officer crossed himself.

'Amazing. You are a true artist, Senor Jiminez, nothing less.'

'One must think of the parents,' Jiminez nodded to his underlings who replaced the lid, raised the coffin once more on the trestle and took it down the steps to the Otter.

The customs officer handed me the documents. 'All would appear to be in order, Senor Nelson. I wish you a safe flight.'

He saluted and moved away and Jiminez glanced up at the sky. 'A perfect night for it if the weather forecast is anything to go by.'

'Let's hope so.' I zipped up my flying jacket. 'I wouldn't like my passenger to have an uncomfortable ride.'

He permitted himself one of those brief graveyard smiles of his. 'You know, I like you, my friend. You have a sense of humour where death is concerned. Not many people do.'

'It takes practice,' I said. 'Lots of practice. I'll be in touch.'

I went down the steps to the Otter where his men had just finished stowing the coffin. I climbed into the cockpit, did the usual routine check, started the engine and ran her down into the water. I took up the wheels and taxied down-wind, leaning out of the side window, checking the channel for boats before making my run.

When the moment came, she lifted like a bird as usual, everything suddenly light and effortless and as I stamped on the right rudder bar and swung out across the quay, Jiminez was still standing down there in the fading light staring up at me. I'd first flown the Otter for a film company who were doing all their location work in Almeria on the Spanish Mediterranean coast for the good and sufficient reason that it's a hell of a sight cheaper than Hollywood these days.

When the film was completed they decided it wasn't worth the expense of having the Otter shipped back to the States. As it became reasonably obvious that no one in the Mediterranean area seemed particularly anxious to buy a floatplane specifically designed to stand the rigours of the Canadian north, they let me have her cheap.

Most people thought I was crazy, but there

was money to be made island-hopping in the Balearics. Ibiza, Majorca, Minorca, Formentera. At least I got by, especially in the season and there were always the extras to help things along, like this present trip, for instance.

It was a fine night, as Jiminez had predicted, with very little cloud and a full moon, stars strung away to the horizon. All very pleasant, but I had more pressing matters on my mind, switched over to automatic pilot and took another look at the chart.

There was no wind to speak of, certainly not more than five knots and I'd allowed for that in my original calculation. There was really very little to be done except to check my figures, which I did, then poured a cup of coffee from a flask and smoked a cigarette.

Thirty-eight minutes out of Cartagena, I took over manual control and went down to two thousand feet. Exactly three minutes later I got my signal right on the button, a blue light followed by a red, flashed half-a-dozen times, some private joke of Turk's who swore it was taken from the old China Coast signal book and meant *I have women on board*.

I went down fast and banked across the boat, a forty-foot diesel yacht from Oran to the best of my knowledge, although the background details were not really my affair. The red light flashed again and I turned away into the wind, eased back on the throttle and started down.

The sea was calm enough and visibility excellent thanks to that full moon. A final burst of power to level out in the descent and I splashed down. I kept the engine ticking over and opened the side door. The motor yacht was already moving towards me. When it was twenty or thirty yards away, it slowed appreciably. I counted four men on deck as usual with another in the wheelhouse. I could see them quite clearly in the moonlight. A rubber dinghy was already in the water by the starboard rail, two of them dropped into it and paddled across.

They drifted in under the port wing and a tall, bearded man in yellow oilskins stepped on to the float, clutching a bulky package against his chest with both hands. He steadied himself for a moment then passed it up to me. As I took it from him, he dropped back into the dinghy without a word and they paddled back to the boat.

I took off again immediately and as I drifted into the air, the boat was already moving away in the general direction of the North African coast. Five minutes later and I was back at three thousand feet and dead on course for Ibiza.

As Turk had said, easy as falling off a log, and each time I repeated the performance we shared two thousand good tax free American dollars.

When I first met Harry Turk he was tied hand and foot to a tree on the edge of a small clearing in the jungle which was being used as a base camp by North Vietnamese regular troops operating behind the American lines. It was raining at the time, which was hardly surprising, as it was the middle of the monsoon season, but in spite of his incredibly filthy condition, I was able to make out that he was a Marine Corps sergeant, as they trussed me up beside him.

Before walking away one of the guards booted me in the side with enough force to crack two ribs, as I later discovered and I writhed around in the mud for a while. I had thought Turk asleep, but now he opened one eye and stared at me unwinkingly.

'What's your story, General?'

I said, 'You've got it wrong. Squadron Leader. What you'd call a major.'

He opened the other eye at that. 'Heh, since when have the British been in this war?'

'They haven't,' I said. 'I did pilot training on a short service commission with the R.A.F. then transferred to the Royal Australian Air Force a couple of years back. This is my second tour out here.'

'What happened?'

'I was hitching a lift on a Medivac helicopter to Saigon out of Din To when we came across a wrecked Huey in the corner of a paddy field with what looked like a survivor waving beside it.'

'So you went down on your errand of mercy and discovered you'd made a big mistake.'

'We were caught in the crossfire of two heavy machine guns. I was the only one who got out in one piece.'

He nodded gravely. 'Well, as my old grannie used to say, you've got to look on the bright side, General, and thank the good Lord. If you'd been taken by the Viet Cong instead of these regular troops they'd have strung you up by your ankles and cut your throat.'

I think it was that remarkable composure of his which impressed me most from the start, for when he closed his eye and went back to sleep, his face, which I could see clearly pillowed on his right arm against the tree trunk, was as serene and untroubled as any child's.

I fell asleep myself in the end in spite of the torrential rain and the cold and awakened again at around three o'clock in the morning to find a hand over my mouth, Turk whispering in my ear as he cut through my bonds. By some means known only to himself, he had managed to break free and had used his belt to garotte the sentry, which gave us an AK assault rifle and a machete between us when we made a run for it.

They were hot on our heels within a matter of hours which was only to be expected and in a brush with a fourman patrol, I took a bullet through the right leg, making me something of a liability from then on. Not that Turk would leave me, even when I did the gallant thing and ordered him to. Not then nor during the five days of hide and seek that followed, until the afternoon we were spotted in a clearing by a Medivac helicopter and winched to safety.

He visited me a couple of times in hospital, but then I was flown back to Australia for treatment. I took my discharge six months later when it became obvious to all concerned that I was going to be left with a permanent limp.

As for Turk, there was a brief period when his face seemed to stare out at me from every magazine and newspaper

I bought which was right after he'd been awarded the Congressional Medal of Honor for leading a party of frogmen into Haiphong harbour to blow up four torpedo boats. I wrote, care of Corps Headquarters in San Diego, but after a while, my letter came back with a note to say he'd taken his discharge and they didn't have any forwarding address.

So that was very much that, until the night I was driving along the Avenida Andenes on the Ibizan waterfront and almost ran over a drunk lying in the middle of the road. Or at least I thought he was drunk until I got out and turned him over and found he was just another hippie, stoned to the eyes.

He had the usual Jesus haircut, a scarlet headband holding it in place, giving him the look of some Apache Indian, an impression reinforced by the lean, ravaged face, deeply tanned by the Ibizan sun.

He wore a linen kaftan and a silver chain belt at his waist, jeans and open sandals. You could have seen dozens like him any day of the week sitting at the tables of the open-air

13

cafes along the waterfront, but in this case there was a significant difference. The Medal of Honor on the end of the silver chain about his neck.

Even then I didn't recognise Turk in this gaunt, ravaged man, until he opened his eyes, gazed up at me unwinkingly in the light of the headlamps and without any kind of surprise at all said gravely, 'And how's every little thing with you, General?'

I didn't live in Ibiza town myself at that time. I was operating out of a tiny fishing village called Tijola on a creek near Port Roig a few miles further along the coast. I didn't need to take Turk home with me as it turned out. He had a boat moored down by the break-water in Ibiza harbour, a thirty-foot seagoing launch, the *Mary Grant*, from which he operated as a freelance skin-diver, although he seldom ventured beyond the Botafoc lighthouse, preferring to earn his bread in more devious ways.

But much of this I was to discover later

and on that first night, I only knew that he had changed almost beyond recognition. That he was a sick man was obvious and when I got him down to the saloon he was barely able to stand.

He sank into a chair, head in hands for a moment, then stood up slowly and leaned on the table. 'You'll have to excuse me for a minute, General, I need an aspirin or something.'

He went into the aft cabin leaving the door slightly ajar, enough for me to see his reflection in a mirror on the cabin wall when I peered in. He had rolled up his left sleeve and was tying a cord around the forearm. As he took a hypodermic from a drawer, I turned away.

He came into the saloon rubbing his hands together briskly, an entirely different person just like the after man in the patent medicine adverts. He took a bottle of brandy from a cupboard and found a couple of reasonably clean glasses.

He pushed one across to me and raised the other in a kind of mock toast. 'To you and me, General,' he said. 'Together again – the old firm.'

And then he started to laugh uproariously.

For a year now he had been going downhill a little bit more each day, slowly being eaten alive by some worm within him. Whatever it was, he never discussed it. He lived entirely in the present moment, blotting out past and future with either a second bottle of whatever came to hand or another fix, involving himself in one vaguely crooked scheme after another.

Like this present affair, for example. When he'd first come to me with the offer I'd turned it down flat thinking it must be drugs, had to be, and that was something I wouldn't have touched if I'd been starving.

But I was wrong for he had got permission from his principals, whoever they were, to open the first package to prove to me that it consisted of dozens of neatly wrapped packets of good American dollar bills. So that was all right. I was just a middle-man, helping to move large sums of money illegally between countries, part of some complicated exchange process by which someone, somewhere, finally made a fortune.

I was still thinking about it all when I made my landfall. I called up the control tower at the airport which was something the authorities insisted I do, in spite of the fact that I didn't use their facilities. There was the usual interminable delay before I was given the all clear to land and turned in to make my final run.

The island looked fantastic in the light of the full moon, the rugged, hilly landscape of the interior like a black paper cut-out against the night sky and a white band of surf showed clearly at the base of the massive south coast cliffs.

I came in off the sea at three hundred feet, Port Roig to the left of me and beyond, between the two great natural granite breakwaters which enclosed the mouth of the creek, I saw the lights of Tijola. A green flare soared into the night giving me the all clear and as I passed between the two headlands, I put the Otter down into calm water and taxied towards the shore.

It wasn't much of a place. A couple of dozen small houses, a jetty, a few fishing boats, but it had everything I needed. Calm water to land in because of the enclosed nature of the creek, and lots of peace and quiet which suited me just fine.

There was a small bar on the beach. I could hear a guitar playing in spite of the Otter's engine, and someone was singing. I dropped the wheels as I moved in towards the beach, and taxied up on to a broad concrete ramp which I'd constructed myself earlier that year with the aid of a couple of locals.

The three men who waited beside the hearse looked exactly the same as the ones I'd left in Cartagena. I switched off the engine, climbed down and they moved past me without a word and started to get the coffin out.

'Heh, General, how did it go?'

I turned round as Turk moved out of the darkness from the general direction of the beach bar. 'Fine. Just fine.'

The three men shuffled past me with the

coffin and I reached into the cabin for the package. I hefted it in my hands for a moment. 'Why don't we just run for the hills with one of these?'

'Don't even think of it.' Turk took the package from me. 'No place to run. Not from these people. They'd leave you with a penny for each eye, that's all.'

'So what is it? Mafia money?'

'Would that bother you?'

'Not particularly. When do we get paid?'

'Thursday. I'll be in touch.' He got into the passenger seat of the hearse and leaned out of the window as the driver started the engine. 'You seeing Lillie tonight?'

'I expect so.'

'You'll find something for her on the table in your kitchen. Give her my love.'

The hearse moved away into the night and I went across the beach to the small flat-roofed cottage I called home. There wasn't much to it. A bedroom, living room and kitchen, with a shower and toilet in the yard at the rear, but it sufficed, at least for the present.

Turk had left the light on in the kitchen. The something he had put on the table turned out to be a thousand American cigarettes, an item which often tends to be in short supply on the island, and a case of Bourbon. Lillie would be pleased. I stripped off quickly, went out to the yard and had a shower.

Lillie was Lillie St Claire. *The* Lillie St Claire, the Queen of the Metro lot for most of her career. Two Oscars and seventy-three movies in all, mostly entirely forgettable, maybe a dozen that had been really worth doing, two that ranked among the best ever.

She'd not made a picture in three or four years now as far as I knew, had dropped out completely and now lived in a kind of feudal splendour in a great white villa on the cliffs above Port Roig. I'd flown her to Majorca one afternoon about six months previously, when she'd missed the scheduled flight and was in a hurry to meet some film producer or other. The acquaintance had ripened into one of those quiet, steady, take-it-or-leave-it affairs which suited us both admirably.

But on a night like this, warm and soft and full of moonlight I looked forward to seeing her with some pleasure. I changed quickly into sweater and slacks, loaded the cigarettes and Bourbon into the rear of the old jeep I kept in the shed out back and drove away.

Lillie's place was seven or eight miles away at the end of a promontory which could only be reached by one of those typically Ibizan dirt roads, twisting and turning between undulating hills, that were more like miniature mountains than anything else, and studded with pine trees.

The night air was heavy with their scent and beyond the cliffs, the sea flashed silver in the moonlight. It was all very spectacular with the Vedra two or three miles or so to my right, a great, solid hump of rock rearing more than a thousand feet out of the sea.

I paused on the brow of the road close to an old ruined mill, a well-known landmark, and got out to admire the view. I reached for a cigarette and somewhere close at hand, a woman screamed, high-pitched and full of terror.

A second later, a naked girl ran out of the darkness into the headlights of the jeep.

2

The Love Goddess

It was as if the camera had stopped turning, freezing the shot for a moment. Dark hair cut very close to the skull – unnaturally short – even the men were wearing it longer that year. Wide eyes above high cheekbones, filled with a kind of calm desperation rather than fear.

And the rest of her, as was to be expected, was calculated to take the breath away. Firm, round breasts, rather small but sharply pointed, the flat belly of a young girl, the hair dark between the thighs.

She came straight into my arms as if unable to stop that head-long flight, clutched at my sweater for a moment then pushed me away with a sudden, desperate cry. I grabbed hold of her by the wrists and held on tight.

'It's all right,' I said. 'It's all right,' then repeated myself in Spanish for good measure.

She went very still, staring up at me, gasping for breath like the hunted animal she was, not saying a word, and a man ran out of the darkness.

Hippies, they will tell you, are God's own chosen people. Flower folk. Gentle souls who only want to drop out of the hell that is modern industrial society. Maybe that was true once when they were content with marijuana, but things have changed since they got on to heroin and L.S.D., and most of the crowd who'd washed up on the shores of Ibiza had drifted up from the bottom of a cess pool in my estimation.

The character who crouched a yard or two away, chest heaving as he fought for breath, was a vintage specimen. His black hair hung well below his shoulders and he wore a plaited leather headband, a scarlet shirt secured by a broad leather belt with a round brass buckle, six inches across, that glowed in the headlights like a small moon. The one incongruous feature were the wire spectacles, the eyes glinting behind them like some malevolent fox, on finding the farmer between him and the chicken.

I didn't need to hear his crazed laugh to know he was as high as a kite or the sight of his shaking hands. It was round about then that two more came crashing out of the pine trees, one of them losing his balance and arriving in an untidy heap in the middle of the road. He got to his feet as the other joined him and they ranged themselves behind Redshirt.

They really were quite something. Identical twins from the look of them and barefooted. Filthy, ragged creatures with tangled beards and long, matted hair, like something out of a child's nightmare about wild men from the woods coming to get you.

Redshirt spread his arms wide and said in a surprisingly soft voice, 'Plenty for everyone, man. You wait your turn is all.'

I said to the girl, 'Get in the jeep. You'll find a reefer jacket in the back.'

As I opened the door for her he came in fast and when he was close enough, I gave him a good, old-fashioned boot in the crutch. In other circumstances it might have killed or crippled him, but the fact that I was only wearing canvas rope-soled sandals took a little of the steam out of things.

In any event, the end result was perfectly satisfactory. He kept on going for a moment, carried forward by the momentum of his own rush, did a rather neat somersault and ended up in the ditch at the side of the road, curled into a very tight ball.

I shoved the girl into the jeep and scrambled in beside her as one of the Terrible Twins howled like a dog and rushed me. I gave him the door full in the face, rammed my foot down hard and took the jeep forward. I had a final impression of the other gibbering like some great ape in the headlights, then he bounced to one side like a rubber ball and we were away.

The girl leaned over the seat, as exciting and disturbing a sight as any man could wish for, and searched vainly in the shadows for the reefer coat. I gave it half-a-mile, just to be on the safe side, then pulled into the side of the road on a small bluff that overlooked the sea. I found the coat, gave it to her then got out of the jeep and walked to the edge of the cliffs. As I lit a cigarette the door slammed behind me. When I turned, the girl was watching me. She'd buttoned the reefer to the neck and turned up the sleeves, but it was still five sizes too large. The contrast between how she now looked and her former condition was incongruous enough to be almost funny.

She came forward, hands in pockets and I offered her a cigarette which she refused. 'Are you all right?' I said.

Her answer was to collapse against me with a long, shuddering sigh. I got an arm around her quickly and held on tight.

After a while, she pulled away. 'Thank you. I'm all right now.' Her English was excellent, but with a pronounced French accent.

I said, 'I'd choose my company a little more carefully another time if I were you.'

She ignored that one and turned to look

out to sea again. 'It is really very beautiful, this world of ours, don't you agree?'

Which, considering what had gone before, was calculated to take the wind out of anyone's sails. But she was right, of course. It was a night to thank God for.

'I know,' I said. 'Where every prospect pleases and only man is vile.'

She looked up at me, frowning slightly. 'You're a strange man. You can be so gentle, yet back there . . .'

'I know, angel,' I said. 'Red in tooth and claw. I served my apprenticeship in a rough school. Of course, I could have passed by on the other side. Would you have preferred that?'

'Please forgive me. I'm being very stupid.' She held out her hand. 'My name is Claire Bouvier and I'm really very grateful.'

I held on to that hand for a moment longer than was strictly necessary, not for romantic reasons, but out of simple curiosity at discovering how work-roughened the palm was. She just didn't look the type.

'Jack Nelson,' I said. 'Was I in time back there?'

28

She took another of those deep breaths. 'Yes, Mr Nelson. You were in time.'

'That's all right then. Where are you staying?'

'A hotel in Ibiza on the Avenida Andenes close to the pier where the boat leaves for Formentera.'

'All right,' I said. 'I've got a friend who has a villa about a mile from here. I'll take you there first, get you some clothes, then I'll take you to your hotel. Or to the police – it's up to you.'

'No – no police.'

The reaction was sharp and definite.

I said, 'Why not? They'd probably run them down without too much difficulty, the state I left them in.'

'No, they've been punished enough.' She was almost angry. 'And it wasn't that kind of assault. It wasn't how it looked. Don't you understand?'

Curiouser and curiouser, and I think she was on the point of telling me more, but I had enough troubles of my own to carry without taking on anyone else's.

'Your affair,' I said. 'Anyway, let's get going.'

I moved to the jeep, opened the door. When I turned she was still standing there at the cliff edge.

'For God's sake,' I said. 'If I'd wanted to rape you I'd have been at it by now. And you're not my type. Thin as a rail and your hair's too short.'

She didn't move an inch. Just stood there looking at me gravely, her face pale in the moonlight. I suddenly had that vaguely helpless feeling one gets on occasions when faced with a stubborn child, intent only on going its own way.

I said as gently as I could, 'All right, you've had a rough night, I understand that, but you've got to start trusting people again. My friend's place is no more than a mile from here and she's a woman so she'll be able to fit you up with some clothes, give you anything you want. You may have heard of her. Her name is Lillie St Claire.'

'The film actress?'

'The very same.'

She came forward slowly, looking suddenly rather forlorn in that ridiculously large reefer coat and held out her hand again. 'Forgive me for doubting you, my friend, but I see now that you are a good man in spite of yourself.'

Speechless and utterly defeated, I climbed in beside her and drove away.

Lillie's place was a typical Ibizencan villa. What the locals called a *finca*, only on a grander scale than most. A great Moorish palace named the Villa Rose built on various levels to fit into the landscape at the end of the point. Castillian arches, iron-grilled windows, the whole so white that in the heat of the day it hurt to look at it.

A high wall surrounded the entire estate, palms nodding beyond, black against the night sky. The great, iron gates were locked tight. The old gnarled peasant who emerged from the hut, complete with Alsatian on a chain, flashed a torch at us.

'It's me, Jose,' I called.

He nodded without a word and returned to the hut, dragging the dog at his heels. A moment later the gates swung open and I drove through.

I could smell the lemon grove although I could not see it, the almond trees and palms swayed gently in the slight breeze, their branches dark feathers against the night sky. And everywhere there was the rattle of water. I pulled in beside the fountain at the bottom of the steps which led up to the great oak front door. When I got out Claire Bouvier joined me reluctantly.

'You don't need to worry,' I said. 'Most of the servants come in during the day. At night there's only an old crone called Isabel who does the cooking and Carlo, the chauffeur.'

She gazed at me blankly. 'She needs a chauffeur at night.'

'You know how it is,' I said. 'No knowing when she might feel like a ride.'

I had pulled the chain at the side of the door and it swung open instantly to reveal Isabel, a gaunt old woman who had never

ever uttered a word in my presence, though whether this was from some personal dislike of me I'd never been able to discover.

She wore traditional dress as always. Blue shawl, a tight-fitting black bodice beautifully embroidered in gold, a black apron worn over the long ankle-length skirt. As usual, she didn't have a thing to say. Not even a flicker of emotion showed on that gnarled old face at the sight of the Bouvier girl, who to Ibizan eyes must have looked eccentric in the extreme.

'Don't look her full in the face or you'll turn to stone,' I told the girl, and I led the way across the wide hall with its beautiful red and white ceramic tiles and mounted a curving staircase to the landing above.

Glass doors stood open to the night and beyond, most of the garden at that level was taken up by a superb illuminated swimming pool. The faithful Carlo was standing beside a wrought-iron table gazing up at the high diving board, a great ox of a man, shoulders bulging beneath the snow-white jacket.

'The Love Goddess,' Claire Bouvier

whispered as she looked up at the slim figure in the black costume poised on the edge of the board.

'That's what they call her,' I said, and as Carlo turned sharply, I raised my voice and cried, 'Heh, Lillie, come down out of there. You've got visitors.'

She waved, then dived a moment later, flashing down through the yellow light, entering the water with hardly a splash. As she surfaced at the side of the pool, Carlo moved in, bathing wrap at the ready. She slipped into it, eyes sparkling, that wide, wide mouth of hers opening into what must surely have been the most devastating smile of all time.

'Why, Jack, lover. It's been an age.' She kissed me, then grabbed an arm reasonably ostentatiously and turned her gaze on Claire Bouvier. 'I didn't know we were having a floor show.'

'Meet Miss Claire Bouvier,' I said. 'I just saved her from a fate worse than you know what back along the road a piece.'

'How perfectly dreadful for you, darling,' Lillie said, managing to sound as if she didn't give a tinker's damn in hell. 'You must tell me all about it down to every last rapacious detail. When you reach my age, you can't afford to miss out on anything. You have a swim or something, lover, I'll see you later.'

'There's a thousand of those foul American fags you like in the back of the jeep.' I said. 'Plus a case of Bourbon. A present from Turk. Shall I bring them in?'

'Good heavens, no. You might pull something mysterious. Ruin your sex life. Leave it to Carlo. He's so much stronger than the rest of us.'

Which was an undeniable fact for I had seen Carlo on occasion, training with weights in the yard by the garage at the back, and stripped he resembled Primo Carnera in his prime. Lillie grabbed the Bouvier girl by the arm and took her inside, Carlo bowed slightly and followed them.

Which left me very much on my own, so I went along to the changing room, found myself a pair of trunks and had a swim.

* * *

The salon was an exquisite room which had been based on an ancient Moorish design. The floor was of black and white ceramic tiles and the ceiling was blue, vivid against stark white walls. A log fire burned on the open hearth. I was sprawled at my ease in front of it, one of Carlo's generously large gin and tonics in my hand, when Lillie came back in.

She really was the most amazing creature I'd ever known. Must have been anywhere up to fifty – had to be to have done the things she had – yet even in the harsh, white heat of the day never seemed to look a day over thirty-five.

Like now, for instance, dressed in a long, black, transparent creation. As far as I could see, she didn't have a stitch on underneath and her legs must have been giving Marlene Dietrich a hard time for years.

She draped herself elegantly across me and kissed me, that mouth of hers opening wide enough to swallow me whole. When the tongue was finally tired of moving around she lay back with a long sigh.

'I've missed you, lover. Where've you been?'

'Working.'

Carlo appeared, a drinks tray in his gloved hands and gave her a martini. She took it just as she accepted the light he held out for her cigarette, as casually as if he didn't really exist. He withdrew silently to a position by the terrace.

She said, 'Where was it these hippies had a go at the kid?'

'Near the mill at La Grande.'

She emptied her glass and paced restlessly across to the fire. 'The dirty bastards. They should drive them off the island, every last one of them.'

'Don't tell me you're frightened?' I said.

She was almost angry when she turned on me. 'What if I am? They've done some funny things. Broken into people's homes. This is a lovely place . . .'

'With Carlo here?' I demanded. 'You've got to be joking. He's the original six-at-one-blow man. I thought that was why you kept him around.'

She changed completely, her face illuminated

by that dazzling smile, the famous Lillie St Claire smile, as she moved across to Carlo.

'That's right. Of course it is. You wouldn't let them hurt me, would you, Carlo?'

Carlo took the hand she held out to him and kissed it gently. From the look on his face I'd say he'd have torn the arms and legs off anyone who even tried.

She patted his cheek. 'Bless you, Carlo. Let's have a movie, shall we? What about *The Door to Hell*.'

He moved away as silently as usual. She poured another drink and flung herself into the chair next to me. This was a ritual I'd been through many times before. There was a small projection room at the rear of the salon and Carlo handled things at that end, using the smooth white wall next to the fireplace as a screen.

As the lights dimmed I said, 'What about the girl?'

'I left her in the bath. She shouldn't be long. Did she tell you how she came to be mixed up with those creeps?'

'I didn't ask.'

'I did. She said she'd arranged to meet a friend at the windmill at La Grande at nine o'clock. She went out there by taxi only he never showed. Then those pigs jumped her.' She shook her head, 'The whole thing stinks to high heaven if you ask me.'

'Her affair, not ours.'

She carried on as if I hadn't spoken. 'And her hair.'

'What about her hair?'

'I don't know. It's not natural. Reminds me of something and I can't think what. A picture I was in once.'

'Why don't you shut up?' I said. '. . . and let's enjoy this one which, for a change, I don't think I've actually seen before.'

I think she'd have given me the hard word at that except for the fact that at that moment, her face filled the screen and as usual, she was swept up in the greatest love affair since Antony and Cleopatra. That of Lillie St Claire for Lillie St Claire.

'1938,' she said. 'I'd been in Hollywood two years. My first Oscar nomination.'

She was standing at the top of a great flight

39

of marble stairs in some sort of negligee or other, being menaced by the swords of half-a-dozen Roundheads, who all looked villainous enough to play Capone-style gangsters, and probably did the following week. At the appropriate moment an athletic-looking character in breeches and a white shirt dropped into the picture, a sword between his teeth and proceeded to knock all sorts of hell out of the Roundheads.

'Jack Desforge,' she breathed. 'The best there ever was.'

'Better than Lillie St Claire?' I demanded.

'Damn you, lover, you know what I mean. Dietrich, Joan Crawford. Oh, they were great. Wonderful, wonderful people. They don't breed them like that any more.'

'Only you were the greatest.'

'Look at my last film.'

'I didn't know anybody had done.'

I ducked to avoid the glass she threw at me for the film was very much a sore point, an Italian production of the worst kind; a programmer which had sunk, as they say, without trace.

Behind us there was a slight polite cough and Claire Bouvier moved down to join us. She wore a pair of slacks and a polo-necked sweater which combined with the short hair to give her a strangely boyish look.

She looked up in some bewilderment at the sword play on the wall then turned to Lillie and said hesitantly, 'You have been most kind, Miss St Claire. I will see these things are returned to you tomorrow.'

'That's all right, darling. You can give them to the deserving poor when you've finished with them.' Lillie told her.

She didn't offer to put her up for the night which was much as I had expected for she was never one for competition in that quarter.

I said to Claire Bouvier, 'All right. Let's get moving.'

She glanced first at Lillie, then at me, strangely diffident, then went up the steps and out into the hall. Lillie said, 'Do you fancy her?'

'I hadn't thought much about it.'

'You'd be making a mistake. There's something funny about that kid.'

41

She slid her arms about my neck and gave the full treatment, following this with a completely unprintable suggestion breathed into my right ear.

'Impossible,' I said.

'Oh, I don't know,' she said. 'We could always try. It shouldn't take you more than an hour to get down to Ibiza town and back again.'

She kissed me hard, that mouth of hers opening wide again and beyond, I saw Carlo waiting respectfully, his face showing no expression worth noting, yet there was something in the eyes I think. I could almost feel the knife going in between my shoulder blades.

I patted her face, 'Perhaps,' I said. 'We'll see,' and I moved out fast.

She didn't have much to say for herself on the way down to town. As we passed the mill where it had all begun I said, 'What in the hell were you doing up here on your own anyway?'

'I had an appointment to keep. With a friend.'

'Who didn't show?' I was surprised at my sudden surge of anger. 'He should have his backside kicked, whoever he is.'

She turned and looked at me sharply, but made no comment. I kept my eyes on the road. After a while she said, 'Tell me about yourself. What do you do?'

'I'm a charter pilot. I keep a floatplane down at Tijola.'

'And Miss St Claire – you have known her long?'

'Long enough.'

We were coming into the outskirts of Ibiza now and I took the direct route in along the Avenida de Espana. There were still plenty of bars open for the night, for Spain at least, was still young, but when I switched off the motor outside the small, waterfront hotel on the Avenida Andenes, it suddenly seemed very quiet.

She got out and moved to the entrance and I followed her. 'I don't suppose you'd feel like a drink?'

'Not really,' she said. 'I'm very tired. You understand?'

'Of course.'

She held out her hand and I took it, suddenly reluctant to let her go.

'What can I say?' she said. 'I owe you so much.'

'You could satisfy my curiosity.'

She thought about it for a long moment then nodded. 'Yes, I owe you that at least. You know the Iglesia de Jesus?'

'One of the most beautiful churches in the island.'

'Can you meet me there in the morning?'

'I think so.'

'Would ten o'clock be too early?'

'I'll be there on the dot.'

She took my hand again briefly. 'Thank you, dear friend,' she said, reached up and brushed my cheek with the lightest of kisses, then slipped inside.

Which very definitely drove every other thought from my mind, including Lillie. There was something elusive about her. Something indefinable that couldn't be pinned down.

Frankly, it was as irritating as an itch one couldn't get at to scratch and irritating in another way also. I had a feeling that I was becoming involved in something in spite of myself and any kind of an entanglement where a woman was concerned, was something I preferred to keep well clear of.

I paused on the edge of the kerb to light a cigarette before crossing to the jeep and an old Ford truck came round the corner on two wheels, mounted the pavement and rushed me like a fighting bull in full charge.

I made it into the nearest doorway with very little to spare, was aware of Redshirt leaning out the cab window laughing like a crazy man and then the truck swerved round the corner into the next street and was away.

I didn't attempt to follow. There'd be another time and I'd had enough action for one night. What I needed now was a long, tall glass of something or other and a cool hand on my fevered brow – which brought me straight back to Lillie.

When I got back to the villa I didn't bother with the front gate, preferring a less public route out of deference to Lillie's good name although I sometimes think she simply liked the idea of someone having to climb over the wall to get to her. As usual, she'd turned the electronic warning system off to facilitate matters.

As I came up out of the garden to the terrace outside her bedroom Lillie called out sharply and it wasn't exactly a cry for help.

The French windows stood open to the night, curtains billowing like white sails and there was a light on inside. Carlo, as far as I could judge, seemed to be performing manfully enough. Certainly a slight, polite cough from the terrace would hardly have helped, so I did the obvious thing and got the hell out of there.

When I got back to Tijola, I stopped at the beach bar and had a large glass of the local brandy, a brew calculated to take the skin off your lips if you were injudicious enough to allow it to touch them. There was a light in the cottage window which didn't surprise me for at that time Turk was in the habit of turning up most nights.

I found him sprawled across the table, out to the wide. The eye balls were retracted, but his pulse was steady enough. Heroin and Spanish Brandy. I wondered how much longer his system was going to be able to take it as I carried him across to the bed.

I covered him with a blanket, turned to go back to the table and saw a piece of paper pinned to the door with the breadknife. *We put the bird to bed for you. Mind your own business in future or next time it's you.*

God knows why I bothered, but I was running when I went out of the door. Not that it mattered because when I reached the slipway, the Otter simply wasn't there.

Definitely not my night.

3

The Jesus Reredos

I was up at first light and drove into Ibiza where I helped myself to a couple of aqualungs and various other essential items of diving gear from the *Mary Grant*.

When I got back to Tijola, Turk was still out cold. I tried slapping him awake which did no good at all and when I attempted to get him on his feet he collapsed instantly, boneless as a jellyfish. It was like handling a corpse and I got him back on the bed and left him to it.

So, I was on my own again – the story of my life, or so it seemed. One thing was certain. Whatever had to be done I would have to do alone so I pulled on one of the yellow neoprene wetsuits I'd brought from the *Mary Grant*, buckled on an aqualung and went to it.

I tried the obvious at first and simply waded into the water from the slipway. The seabed shelved very rapidly at that point so that it was four or five fathoms deep close inshore.

The water was like black glass, giving the illusion of being quite clear and yet visibility was poor, mainly because the sun wasn't yet out.

I went out, as I have said, in a direct line from the slip-way for perhaps fifty yards, keeping close to the bottom and didn't see a thing. So I tried another approach and moved back towards the shore, tacking twenty yards to either side of my central line in a slow, painful zig-zag.

Which all took time – too much time. I hadn't eaten, hadn't even swallowed a cup of coffee which was a mistake for, in spite of the wetsuit, it was cold.

I was getting old, that was the trouble. Too old for this kind of nonsense. The cold ate into me like acid and I was gripped by a mood of savage despair. Everything I had in the world was tied up in the Otter. Without it I was nothing. On the beach once and for all and no way back.

I surfaced close to the slipway and found Turk sitting cross-legged on the beach, a blanket around his shoulders. There was a bottle of that cheap local brandy wedged in the sand between his feet and he nursed a tin cup in both hands.

'Enjoying yourself?' he asked.

'The only way to live.'

He swallowed some more of that terrible brandy and nodded slightly, a curiously vacant look in his eyes. It was as if he was not really there, in spirit at least.

He said, 'Okay, General, what's it all about?'

So I told him. The mill at La Grande, Claire Bouvier, Redshirt and his friends – the whole bit and as I talked, the sun edged its way over the point, flooding the creek with light.

When I was finished he shook his head

51

and sighed heavily. 'You never did learn to mind your own business did you? Little friend of all the world.'

'That's me,' I said. 'Now let's have your professional opinion.'

'Simple. You've been looking in the wrong place. The way the currents run in this cove you should have tried the mid-channel.'

My heart, as they say, sank. 'But it's fifteen or sixteen fathoms in places out there.'

'I know, General. I know.' He smiled wearily. 'Which is why you're going to need papa. Give me five minutes to get into my gear. We'll use the inflatable with the outboard and make sure there's at least twenty fathoms of line on the anchor. We're going to need it out there.'

I said, 'Are you sure you feel up to this?'

'You've got to be joking,' he replied without even an attempt at a smile.

He turned and walked away with a curious kind of dignity, the blanket trailing from his shoulders like a cloak and yet there was something utterly and terrifyingly wrong. Earlier when I had attempted to waken him he had

seemed like a corpse. Now the corpse walked.
It was simple as that.

I was crouched in the dinghy in mid-channel
taking a breather just before nine o'clock
when Turk surfaced and gave me the sign. I
adjusted my mouthpiece, went over the side
and followed him down through around ten
fathoms of smoke-grey water.

The Otter was crouched in a patch of
seagrass like some strange marine monster.
From a distance everything seemed perfectly
normal and then, when I was close enough,
I saw the holes ripped in the floats and hull.

So that was very much that and there was
certainly nothing to hang around for. I
followed Turk up and surfaced beside the
dinghy. He spat out his mouthpiece and
grinned savagely.

'Somebody's a handy man with a fireaxe.
You certainly know how to win friends and
influence people.'

I pulled myself into the dinghy, unstrapped
my aqualung and started the outboard.

'All right, so I'm splitting my sides laughing. What are the prospects?'

'Of raising her?' He shrugged. 'Oh, I could do it, but I'd need to have a couple of pontoons and a steam winch and we'd need to recruit half-a-dozen locals as general labourers.'

'How long?'

'A month – maybe more if the weather plays us up, but whatever happens it would cost you. Four, maybe five thousand dollars and that would be cutting it to the bone, a friend for a friend.'

Which still left repairs to the floats and hull and the entire engine would have to be stripped, the control system. And add to that the airworthiness check the authorities would insist on before she flew again. God alone knows how much that would cost.

'Is it on?' he asked.

I shook my head. 'Not in a thousand years.'

'What about insurance?'

'Nothing that would cover this. I could never afford the right kind of premium.'

I killed the motor as we drifted in through

the shallows and we got out and pulled the dinghy up onto the beach together.

Turk picked up his aqualung. 'This character in the red shirt and wire glasses. I'll ask around. Somebody must know him.'

'What good would that do?' I said bitterly. 'He could never pay for this.'

'Maybe not, but you could always take it out of his hide some, after asking him politely why he did it?'

I suppose it was only then that the full extent of the catastrophe really got through to me and I kicked out at the inflatable dinghy savagely.

'Why?' I said. 'Why?'

'I'd say the girl was the person to put that question to.'

'Claire Bouvier?'

'She didn't want the police in on things did she? She told you it wasn't how it looked. This creep tried to run you down in a truck and failing in that direction, sees the Otter off and leaves you a warning to mind your own business. I'd say if anyone can throw any light on the situation it should be her.'

I glanced at my watch. It was just after nine-thirty. 'Okay, that makes sense if nothing else does. I've arranged to meet her at ten o'clock at the Iglesia de Jesus. You want to come along for the ride?'

He smiled, that strange, melancholy smile of his. 'Not me, General, I haven't been to church in years. It's not my scene and neither is this. I've got my own coffin to carry. You're on your own.'

And on that definite and rather sombre note, he turned and walked into the cottage.

The Iglesia de Jesus is no more than a ten-minute drive from the town and stands in the middle of some of the richest farmland in Ibiza. An area criss-crossed with irrigation ditches, whitewashed farmhouses dotting a landscape that is strikingly beautiful. Lemon groves and wheatfields everywhere, even palm trees combining with the Moorish architecture of the houses to paint a picture that is more North African than European.

The church itself is typical of country

churches to be found all over the island. Beautifully simple in design, blindingly white in the Mediterranean sun. A perfect setting for one of the most glorious pieces of Gothic art in Europe.

When I opened the door and went inside it was like diving into cool water. The silence was so intense that for a moment, I paused as if waiting for something though I hadn't the slightest idea what. A sign perhaps, from heaven to tell me that everything was for the best in this best of all possible worlds. That my own experience of life and its rottenness was simply an illusion after all.

There was the usual smell of incense, candles flickered down by the altar. There was no one there, and I suddenly knew with a kind of anger, that the girl wasn't going to come. Had never intended to.

And then I saw that I had been mistaken in thinking I had the place to myself for a nun in black habit knelt in front of the Reredos, head bowed, hands clasped in prayer.

I took a deep breath, fought hard to

contain the impulse to kick out at something and made for the door.

A soft, familiar voice called, 'Mr Nelson.'

I turned slowly, too astounded to speak.

The central panel of the Jesus Reredos portraying the Virgin and Child is a masterpiece by any standard and beautiful in the extreme. But it is an austere beauty. Something quite untouchable by anything human with the quiet serenity of one who knows that God is Love beyond any possibility of doubt and lives life accordingly.

Standing in front of it in that simple, black habit, Claire Bouvier might well have been mistaken for the artist's model had it not been for the fact that the Reredos had been painted in the early years of the sixteenth century.

It could only be for real – had to be – I didn't doubt that for a minute, for in some strange way it fitted. At least it explained the cropped hair and I sat down rather heavily in the nearest pew.

'I am sorry, Mr Nelson,' she said. 'This must be something of a shock for you.'

'You can say that again. Why didn't you tell me last night?'

'The cirumstances were unusual to say the least as I think you will agree.'

She sat down rather primly in the chair next to me, hands folded in her lap, those work-roughened hands which had so puzzled me. Then she looked up at the Reredos.

'I didn't realise it was so beautiful. Everything is so moving – so perfectly part of a whole. Particularly the scenes from the life of the Virgin on the predella.'

'To hell with the . . .' She turned sharply and I took a deep breath and continued. 'Look, what do I call you for a start?'

'I am still Claire Bouvier, Mr Nelson. Sister Claire, if you prefer it, of the Little Sisters of Pity. I'm on leave from our convent near Grenoble.'

'On leave?' I said. 'Isn't that a little irregular?'

'There are special circumstances. I've been in East Pakistan for the past couple of years or BanglaDesh as they now call it.'

The whole thing seemed to move further

into the realms of fantasy by the minute. I said, 'All right, just tell me one thing. You were dressed like a nun last night when our friends grabbed you?'

'That's right.'

'And you said it wasn't just an ordinary assault. You wouldn't let me take you to the police, for instance, which I would have thought reasonably strange behaviour for someone of your persuasion.'

She got up abruptly, moved towards the altar and stood there gripping the rail. I said quietly, 'Our friend in the red shirt tried to run me down in a truck last night after I left you. When I got back to my cottage at Tijola, I found a note telling me to mind my own business.'

She turned quickly, a frown on her face. 'From whom?'

'Redshirt and friends. It has to be. You'll be interested to know they also towed my seaplane out into the middle of the channel and sank it in sixty feet of water, just to encourage me.'

There was genuine horror on her face at

that, but she turned away again, head bowed, gripping the rail so tightly that her knuckles whitened.

I grabbed her by the shoulders and turned her round roughly. 'Look, that plane was all I had in the world and it's not salvageable, so I'm finished, Sister. A ruined man because I played the Good Samaritan last night. At least I'm entitled to know why.'

She looked up at me calmly without struggling and nodded. 'You are right, dear friend. I owe you that at least. Perhaps there is a quiet place you know of? Somewhere we could talk . . .'

I took the road to Talamanca then followed a cart track that brought us after a couple of miles to an old ruined farmhouse in an olive grove above the sea. There wasn't a soul around. She sat on a low stone wall which had once marked the boundary of the grove and I sprawled on the ground at her feet and smoked a cigarette.

It was a marvellous day and quite suddenly,

nothing seemed to matter very much. I narrowed my eyes, watching a hawk spiralling down out of the blue and she said, 'Did you really mean what you said back there in the church? That you are ruined?'

'As near as makes no difference.'

She sighed, 'I too, know what it is like to lose everything.'

'Is that supposed to make me feel better?'

She looked down at me sharply, something very close to anger in her face for the first time, but she controlled it admirably.

'Perhaps if I told you about it, Mr Nelson.'

'Has it anything to do with this present affair?'

'Everything.' She plucked a green leaf from a caper shrub, shredding it between her fingers as she stared back into the past. 'I was born in Algeria. In the back country. My father was French, my mother, Bedu.'

'An interesting mixture,' I said. 'Where do you keep your knife?'

She ignored me completely and carried straight on. 'We had a large estate. Two vineyards. My father was a wealthy man.

When de Gaulle declared Algeria independent in 1962 we decided to stay, but by 1965 things were very bad. All agricultural land owned by foreigners had been expropriated and most of the French population had gone. When my mother died, my father decided it was time we left also.'

'How old were you then?'

'Just fourteen. He decided to fly us out secretly, mainly because he considered it unlikely that the authorities would allow us to leave with anything worth having.'

'There was another reason?'

'I think you could say that.' She smiled faintly. 'There was a convent of the Little Sisters of Pity not far from our place at Tizi Benou. An old Moorish palace built like a fortress. I received my education there. During those difficult early years of independence, it acted as a refuge many times and churches over the entire region sent their more tangible assets there for safe keeping rather than see them looted.'

The whole thing was beginning to sound more than interesting and I sat up and turned to face her. 'These tangible assets – what exactly did they consist of?'

'Oh, the usual things. Church plate, precious objects of various kinds. Most of this was rendered down into bullion at the convent, crudely, but effective enough.'

'Why bullion?' It was something of a super-fluous question for I already knew the answer.

'So that my father could fly it out.'

'And how much did that little lot come to?'

'Something over a million pounds sterling in gold and silver. A rough approximation only and then there was a considerable amount in precious stones impossible to estimate and the most important item of all was priceless.'

'And what was that?'

'A statue of the Virgin in beaten silver, known as Our Lady of Tizi Benou, but actu-ally manufactured by the great Saracen silversmith, Amor Khalif in Damascus in the eleventh century.'

'My God, but they must have loved you when you flew in with that little lot.' I said.

'But we didn't, Mr Nelson,' she said calmly. 'That's the whole point. It's still there.'

'The pilot my father hired was a man named Jaeger. A South African. He flew in from France by night at four hundred feet. He told me that was to foil their radar.' She shook her head and there was a kind of sadness in her voice. 'He was so alive. A great, black-bearded man who seemed to laugh all the time and wore a pistol in a shoulder holster. I think he was the most romantic figure I'd ever seen in my life.'

'What was the aircraft?'

'A Heron, is that right?'

I nodded, 'Four engines. They used them for the Queen's Flight a few years back. What about passengers?'

'My father and I and Talif who was overseer of the vineyards.'

'What was his story?'

'He had worked for my father for years. They were very close.' She shrugged. 'He preferred to come with us rather than stay.

There should have been others, but there was trouble at the last moment and we had to leave in a hurry.'

'What went wrong?'

'Oh, I don't really know. Somehow the local area commander got to know – Major Taleb. He and my father never really got on. Taleb's mother had been French, but for some reason that only seemed to make him hate France more. He'd fought with the F.L.N. for years.'

'What happened?'

'We took off as Taleb arrived to arrest us. Not that it did us any good. I suppose he must have got on to their air force straight-away.'

'And you were intercepted?'

She nodded. 'Over the Algerian coast near Cape Djinet. Are you familiar with that coast at all? Do you know the Khufra Marshes?'

'I've heard of them.'

'Jaeger managed to crash-land and in one of the lagoons in there. He and my father were killed and the Heron went to the bottom, but Talif managed to get me out in time.

He took me to a fishing village not far away, a place called Zarza and nursed me back to health. Later, he got me to France and placed me in the care of the Little Sisters at Grenoble.'

'And did you tell anyone about all this?'

'Only the Sisters, but there was nothing to be done about the situation obviously. To the Algerians, of course, we were all dead.'

'So what happened then?'

'The Order used its influence to get Talif work in Marseilles. I continued my education with them and eventually realised I had a vocation. After my training as a nurse, they sent me to our centre in Dacca.'

'And now you're back.'

'For a time only. I had yellow fever very badly. It was thought that a spell in Grenoble would prove beneficial.'

Which was all absolutely fascinating, but came nowhere near explaining more recent events.

'So what's all this got to do with Redshirt and his friends?' I demanded.

'That's simple enough. They work for

Taleb. He's a colonel now in the Algerian Security Police. I've made enquiries.'

'But how in the hell did he come back into the picture?'

'Talif came to see me in Grenoble three weeks ago. It seems that about a month ago while working on the Marseilles docks, he was recognised by an Algerian merchant navy officer he'd known years before. He packed his bags at once and moved to Lyon where he got work on the night shift at the local market. When he got home one morning, he found Taleb waiting for him in his room. He told Talif that if he came back to Algeria with him and showed them where the plane had gone down, they'd give him ten per cent and a government job.'

'And what did Talif do?'

'Pretended to agree, then gave him the slip on the way to Marseilles and came to see me.' She raised her hands and suddenly her face was flooded by the most glorious smile imaginable. 'Oh, how can I put it to you. It seemed like a sign. Like something that was meant to be.'

I was completely puzzled. 'I don't understand.'

'Our hospital in Dacca was burned to the ground, Mr Nelson. We lost everything. We have willing hands, plenty of those, but now what we need more than anything else in the world is money.'

I saw it all then, in that single, precise moment in time and stared at her in astonishment. 'And you think the best way of raising it is to pay a quick visit by night to the Khufra Marshes.'

'Exactly,' she said, her eyes shining. 'When Mr Jaeger was dying, just before the plane sank he gave me the exact bearing, made me repeat it to him. It's burned into my brain until this very day.'

'What do the Sisters of Pity think of this little scheme?'

'They know nothing about it. I was due some leave and I'm taking it. Talif agreed to help and we decided, between us, that Ibiza would be the most suitable base for operations. It's only two hundred miles from here to Cape Djinet. I borrowed a little money from an old aunt in Dijon and Talif came on ahead of me to procure a suitable boat.'

'You must be stark, staring, raving mad,' I said.

'Not at all. Talif wrote to tell me he had arranged for a boat and was negotiating with a diver. He suggested I join him this week and booked a hotel room for me.'

'Let me get this straight,' I said. 'You actually intend to go with him?'

'Naturally.'

The whole thing by then, of course, had assumed all the aspects of a privileged nightmare and I was aware of that curiously helpless feeling again where she was concerned.

I said, 'All right, what about Redshirt and his pals last night.'

'There was a note from Talif at the hotel when I got in yesterday. It asked me to meet him at the Mill at La Grande at nine o'clock. It seemed genuine enough. I went out there by taxi.'

'And promptly found yourself in the bag.'

To my astonishment she said, 'They were

not responsible for their actions, those young men. They were all under the influence of drugs.'

'Oh, I get it,' I said. 'I suppose I hit them too hard. Anyway, how can you be sure they weren't just three fun-loving boys out for kicks?'

'Because they had an argument about keeping me intact, as the one in the red shirt termed it, for Taleb.'

'In other words, things just got out of hand?'

'I suppose so.'

'And Talif?'

'Not a word. He gave me no address. Simply told me that he would contact me through the hotel.'

Which didn't look too good for Talif.

I said, 'So what are you going to do now?'

'I don't know. Look for him, I suppose.' She hesitated, glanced at me rather shyly, then looked down at her hands. 'It's a great imposition I know, Mr Nelson, but I was wondering whether you might be persuaded to help me.'

'To go into the Khufra Marshes?' I demanded. 'You must be joking.'

She held up a hand defensively. 'Of course not. I simply want to find Talif, that's all, and it occurred to me that with your local knowledge, you might be able to help.'

The face, framed by the white band of her hood, was as guileless as any child's. I sighed heavily, got to my feet and gave her a hand up.

'All right, Sister, I'll find Talif for you. It should be simple enough. Algerians aren't exactly thick on the ground in Ibiza. But that's all – understood?'

'Perfectly, dear friend,' she said with that calm, radiant smile of hers, turned and led the way back to the jeep.

I followed a trifle reluctantly, I admit, but when it came right down to it, I didn't really seem to have much choice – or did I?

The hotel she was staying at was decent enough. Little more than a pension really and it was certainly no tourist trap. Quiet and unpretentious. I could see why Talif had chosen it. There was no one behind the desk in the tiny entrance hall and when I rattled the brass handbell it sounded unnaturally loud in the quiet.

'I tried to make some enquiries about Talif this morning,' Sister Claire whispered. 'But I didn't get very far. The proprietor only seems to speak Spanish and half a dozen words of English.'

A door at the back opened and a fat, amiable man appeared in a straw hat and green baize apron. From the trowel in his hand it seemed a fair assumption that he had been gardening.

He removed his hat instantly, not for me, but for Sister Claire, a slightly anxious smile on his face. It seemed more than likely that the language difficulty had been a great worry to him.

'Ah, senor,' I said in Spanish. 'Perhaps you could help us?'

The relief on his face was intense and he bobbed his head eagerly. 'At your orders, senor.'

'The good Sister is anxious to contact her friend. The one who booked the room for her. Unfortunately she has mislaid his address and as her time is strictly limited . . .'

'Ah, the Arab, senor.' He shrugged. 'What can I say? He left no address with me.'

I turned to Sister Claire who waited anxiously, 'It's no go, I'm afraid.'

And then the proprietor added, 'Of course, I have seen this man on many occasions, senor.'

'And where would that be?'

'Pepe's place at the other end of the harbour by the breakwater. You know it, senor?'

'My thanks.'

We went out into the heat of noon. There was a small cafe next to the hotel, tables and chairs spilling across the sidewalk.

'Did he tell you anything?'

'Only that Talif's been in the habit of using a certain bar at the other end of the water-front. I'll go and see what I can dig up there.'

'Can't I come with you?'

I shook my head. 'Not your style at all, Sister. The sort of place stevedores and sailors use. They'd run for the hills if a nun walked in. You have a coffee and admire the view.'

I steered her firmly towards a table under a large and colourful umbrella, snapped my fingers for a waiter and was away before she could argue.

She was on her second cup when I got back, the waiter hovering, anxiously a table to two away, for Ibizans, like all Spaniards, have enormous respect for anything to do with the Church.

She looked up eagerly. 'Did you get anywhere?'

'I think you could say that.' I told the waiter to bring me a gin and tonic and sat down. 'The man who owns the place, Pepe, had arranged to hire Talif a thirty-foot sea-going launch and he was trying to find him a diver.'

'And Talif?'

'Pepe hasn't seen him for the last couple of days, but he was able to tell me where he's been staying. It seems Talif wanted somewhere cheap and quiet so Pepe arranged for a cousin of his to rent him an old cottage in the hills near Cova Santa.'

'Is it far?'

'No more than half-an-hour.'

She didn't even ask if I would take her, simply pushed back her chair, stood up and waited for me to make a move with obvious impatience.

I swallowed the rest of my gin and tonic hurriedly. 'Don't I even get to eat, Sister?'

She frowned in obvious puzzlement. 'I don't understand, Mr Nelson.'

I sighed as I took her elbow. 'Take no notice, Sister. Just my warped sense of humour. Lead on by all means and let us be about the Lord's business.'

We drove out of town following the main road to San Jose. As was to be expected at that time of day, we had things pretty much to ourselves, the locals having the good sense to get in out of the fierce noonday heat.

She didn't say a word until we were through Es Fumeral and then she said suddenly, as if trying to make conversation, 'This Cova Santa you mentioned. What is it? Another village?'

I shook my head. 'Some underground caverns. A big tourist attraction. The mugs roll up by the bus load during the season to see the stalactites by electric light. Then they're invited to take part in a barbecue, for which they've already paid handsomely. Roast sucking pig and plenty of cheap wine. And I mustn't forget the exhibition of folk dancing in national costume. They'll even allow you to take part. A wonderful chance to experience something of the simple joys of peasant life.'

She turned to look at me and I kept my eyes on the road. 'You hate life then, Mr Nelson, or just people?'

I was angry, touched on the raw, I suppose, and showed it. 'What in the hell is this supposed to be – confession? Three Hail Marys, two Our Fathers and be a good boy in future.'

She turned to look at me, no anger in her at all, only a slight frown of enquiry and then she sighed, the breath going out of her in a dying fall.

'Ah, I see what it is. Now I see. It is only yourself you hate. Now why should that be?'

But now we were close to the dangerous edge of things – too close for comfort.

I said warmly. 'I'll go to hell in my own way, Sister, like all men. Let's leave it at that.'

I put my foot down hard and took the jeep away at the kind of speed which made any further conversation impossible.

About a mile up the Cova Santa road and still following Pepe's instructions I turned left into a cart track and climbed into the hills.

On the lower slopes there was a farm or two, terraces of almonds and wheat still in its young growth, but we climbed higher into a wilder terrain of jagged peaks and narrow, tortuous ravines, stunted pines carpeting the slopes.

We had not spoken for some time, but now she said, 'What exactly are we looking for?'

'A tumbledown cottage and a disused mill, about two miles along this track on the right according to Pepe.'

'Then I think we are here.'

There was a flash of white through the

pine trees. I dropped a gear as the road started to climb around a great outcrop of rock. On the other side it petered out in a clearing among the trees. There was a crumbling stone wall, the usual arched entrance typical of Ibizan farmhouses.

The yard was choked with weeds and an old cart which leaned against the wall minus one wheel had poppies growing all over it. The house badly needed a fresh coat of white-wash as did the stump of the mill, which stood beside it minus its sails.

I switched off the engine and we sat there, the only sound steam hissing gently as it escaped from the radiator filler cap for the steep climb in that great heat had taken its toll of the old jeep.

'If he was here he'd have been out by now,' I said stating the obvious, but being also careful to omit another quite possible reason for his non-appearance.

Her disappointment showed plain enough. She seemed near to tears and I suddenly felt sorry for her, yet irritated at the same time that she could so move me.

'You wait here while I look things over,' I told her and got out of the jeep.

The plain truth is, of course, that I just didn't want her around in case I discovered something unpleasant, which seemed more than likely in view of recent events plus the fact that Talif hadn't been seen around for a couple of days.

The front door opened to my touch, almost fell off, in fact, for it was secured by one hinge. The living room contained only an old pinewood table. The two bedrooms held nothing – nothing at all and the entire place had that air of general neglect that comes from long disuse. When I returned to the living room, Sister Claire was standing by the fireplace.

I said, 'No sign of him and no sign that he's even been here.'

She pointed to the hearth. 'There's been a fire here recently.'

Which was true enough. 'All right, there's still the mill.'

But I drew a blank there also for the door obviously hadn't been opened in years and when I touched it, it simply fell down. Inside there were a few items of old machinery, rusting into the ground and coated with the dust of many years and the stairs to the upper storey had long since rotted away.

I turned and found her hovering in the doorway anxiously. I shook my head. 'Nothing here, I'm afraid.'

I followed her out into the bright sunlight and when we got to the jeep she paused, her back towards me. When she turned, her face was calm, but there was a question in her eyes.

'You think something has happened to him, don't you?'

'All right,' I said, 'since you're asking. It seems to me there are two possibilities. The first is that he's gone to ground after realising that Taleb was snapping at his heels.'

'And is quite simply afraid to show his face?'

'Exactly.'

'But you don't think that?'

'I'd say it's more than likely he's at the bottom of the harbour with about fifty pounds of chain about his ankles.'

What happened then was interesting and certainly had nothing to do with Talif. An expression of extreme desperation appeared on her face and she turned and hammered the edge of the canvas tilt in a kind of frustration.

When she spoke it was in a kind of hoarse whisper. 'What am I going to do? There's so little time.' She turned to face me, quite distraught and added brokenly, 'Talif had everything. All my money.'

'I'm sorry,' I said.

'Are you?' Her expression changed, hardened, and there was a sudden glint in her eye. 'All I need is a boat, Mr Nelson and a diver.'

'And how would you pay him?'

'On our return.'

'Oh, I see, you'd give him a share.'

She frowned at that. 'An agreed amount should be sufficient. I would offer a suitable contract.'

I could hardly believe my ears, 'For services rendered, you mean?' I laughed harshly. 'You've got to be joking. Wait for me here. I'll see if I can find some water for the jeep.'

She grabbed me by the sleeve and pulled me round. 'You must know someone. Someone with a suitable boat. The kind of man who would be willing to take such a chance.'

Which I did, of course, and remembering, laughed out loud. 'All right,' I said. 'And what if I do? What if I tell you I've got a friend who not only has a very suitable boat, but also happens to be the best diver in this part of the Mediterranean? What's in it for me?'

She stared up at me, the eyes very blue, the face calm again. 'Mr Nelson, the lives of a great many people may depend upon the speed with which we can rebuild our hospital in Dacca . . .'

I put up a hand and cut her dead. 'All right, you win. I've got a friend in Ibiza called Harry Turkovich – an American. You may find him a trifle eccentric, but he's everything else I said he was. I'll take you to see him this afternoon. What happens after that is between the two of you. Ask me for help again and I'll run for the hills.'

'God bless you,' she said, a remark that from anyone else would have been enough to make me puke and yet from her, it sounded right because she meant it.

I was like a drowning man going down for a third time and I hastily disengaged myself from the hand she put on my sleeve. 'I'll see about that water,' I muttered and fled.

There was an old draw-well in the rear yard enclosed in a beehive structure of solid grey stone, the kind you could walk inside.

There was a trough ready filled with water and an old bucket. There was also a rather unpleasant smell from the well. I peered outside quickly to make sure Sister Claire hadn't followed me then I grabbed the handle and started to wind up the rusting chain which hung down into the darkness.

It took all my strength which told its own story. The smell, when he finally appeared, was overpowering. He was hanging by his ankles, head-down. From the looks of things I'd say they'd been trying to make him talk. I lowered him back down, my arms aching from the strain, then I filled the bucket from the trough and went out into the clean air.

I paused to light a cigarette, leaning against the wall of the well for a moment. I suppose I knew then that I wasn't going to tell her because if I did, she would have no alternative but to go to the police . . .

And that wouldn't do at all, I suddenly realised that. I thought of Talif down there in the well. No one could help him now. I also thought of the Heron on the bottom of that lagoon in the Khufra Marshes. Had been thinking of it for longer than I cared to admit, I suppose. What had she said? *A million at least in gold and silver plus God knows how much in precious stones.*

I went back to the jeep, walking briskly and topped up the radiator. There was just one thing, however. One thing I had to know.

As I climbed behind the driving wheel I said casually, 'Just how much information would your friend Talif have to give anyway?'

'About the position of the plane, you mean?' She shook her head. 'I am the only one who knows that. We crashed by night remember and wandered in the marsh for two days before reaching the village. It's like a lost world in there. Everything looks the same.' As I started the engine she added, 'Why do you ask?'

'Well, it's a point, angel, isn't it?' I said and drove away quickly.

4

The Gate of Fear

I tried the most obvious place for Turk first, the *Mary Grant*, but there was no sign of him. Everything was in its usual neat and tidy condition – what old-time sailors would have termed shipshape and Bristol fashion. I could never make up my mind whether this was simply a case of Marine training or whether there was some deeper, psychological reason. An attempt, perhaps, to hang on to some shred of order and decency when every other thing in his life was squalor and decay.

When I went back up the twenty-foot iron ladder to the breakwater, Sister Claire leaned over anxiously. 'Isn't he there?'

'I'm afraid not.'

'Then where will he be? It's a question of time now, Mr Nelson. You must surely see that.'

'He could be in any one of a dozen bars for a start.' I said. 'And if I can't find him there, there are establishments of another kind. You follow me?'

'I am not a child, Mr Nelson,' she said as we started along the breakwater to where I'd left the jeep. 'Strange how many people automatically assume that nuns and priests must be unworldly people, completely cut off from the realities of life.'

'Fair comment, I would have thought.'

'Has it ever struck you that a parish priest has more sin and degradation poured into his ear in a week than the average sinner manages to come across in a lifetime?'

I said, 'I didn't think nuns took confessions.'

'They don't, but we make up for it in other ways. During my last year in Dacca before the war broke out, I was in charge of a ward dealing solely with syphilitics. A salutary experience.'

'I can believe that.'

We had reached the jeep and as I handed her in she said briskly, 'Now then, what about Mr Turkovich?'

'Turk,' I said. 'Everybody calls him Turk. You'd better leave that to me. I'll see if I can run him down while you have some lunch, but it could take time.'

'All right,' she said as we drove away. 'Now what can you tell me about him? What should I know?'

'You want it straight?'

She looked surprised. 'But of course.'

'All right. For a start he's a dying man because he doesn't want to live.'

'Do you mean that seriously?'

'Oh, yes, a little bit more each day. Cheap brandy and drugs. He picked up the habit in Vietnam. He was an underwater specialist with the marines. A Medal of Honor man. Have you any idea what that means?'

'Yes, I think so. He must be a very brave man.'

'I know one thing – he's changed since I first met him. Something's eating him alive though God knows what it is.'

'You were in Vietnam also?' She looked puzzled. 'But you are English.'

'I flew with the Australian Air Force,' I said. 'Didn't you know a couple of Victoria Crosses have been awarded to Australians in Vietnam? Surprising how many people don't realise that.'

I pulled up outside the hotel and handed her down. She paused on the steps before going inside and looked at me seriously.

'Do you think there's a chance he might be interested?'

'I don't see why not,' I said. 'A suitable enterprise for a dying man.'

She hesitated and I knew what was coming before she said it. 'And you, Mr Nelson. Would you consider joining us if the terms were right?'

'It's certainly a thought,' I said. 'On the other hand, my old Scottish grannie used to tell me when I was a lad that I'd been blessed with good sense.'

And as usual, I got out of it fast before she could reply.

* * *

Trying to run Turk to earth was a frustrating occupation, but as good a way of passing the time as any, especially if you had a couple of days to spare.

I tried half-a-dozen bars along the water-front without success then moved into the labyrinth of the Sa Penya quarter which meant leaving the jeep because the streets were so narrow they could only be negotiated on foot.

When I'd exhausted every possibility in that area, I moved on to the Dalt Vila, the oldest part of Ibiza, the old high town, still entirely surrounded by massive walls built in the 16th century. It's an imposing sight, especially from a distance when you can't smell the drains; tall white moorish houses crammed in together on the hillside, their roofs rising in steps to the cathedral of Santa Maria.

All very picturesque, but I had other things on my mind. I climbed high into the old Moorish quarter, sweat soaking my shirt, trying to ignore the stench of urine and human excrement that seemed so all pervading and looked for him at a small discreet establishment that was a whorehouse in all but name.

They hadn't seen him in a week which seemed unlikely and as I went back down through the narrow streets my bad leg was beginning to hurt like hell. I dropped into a chair at the first pavement cafe I came to and called for a beer.

The waiter who brought it knew me well. 'A fine day, Senor Nelson. Your friend was here earlier.'

As simple as that. I said, 'How long ago?'

'A couple of hours. Maybe more.'

'Any idea where he went?'

'He asked me to phone for a taxi. When it came, I heard him ask the driver to take him to Esponja.'

Which could only mean one thing. I got up quickly and he put a hand on my sleeve. 'Senor, let me warn you. He is in one of his black moods with much drink taken.'

'How much?'

'Nearly a full bottle of brandy while he was here.'

Which put something of a damper on things for Turk in one of those moods and with that kind of drink taken was capable of almost anything. I thanked the waiter and moved out fast.

Esponja was a hamlet on the coast not far from my own place at Tijola and, where Turk was concerned, it could only mean one thing. Big Bertha.

She was a Dutch girl who'd arrived on the island a few months earlier with a new influx of hippies. Most of them lived in communes, changing partners with the frequency of dancers doing the Paul Jones, but Bertha was her own woman. When she wanted a man, she had one in and she never needed to ask twice. The rest of the time she lived in a decaying farmhouse on the cliffs at the end of the worst road in the world and painted.

As far as Turk was concerned she was the greatest thing in bed since the Goddess Kali. The great Earth Mother and the wisest woman in the world rolled into one and he usually ran to sit at her feet, whenever the world moved in on him.

When I braked to a halt in the yard of the

old farmhouse there was nobody about, but her car, a small Seat 750 saloon was parked inside the barn. I hammered on the door, but there was no reply so I followed a path round to the cliff edge and looked down to the beach.

There was a towel spread on the sand by some rocks and an easel stood beside it, a half-painted canvas in position. Of Bertha there was no sign. I went down the path quickly and as I dropped into the soft white sand, she came round the point at the gallop mounted on a piebald horse.

She rode bareback which was in keeping for as far as I could see, the only thing she was wearing was a long scarlet headband to hold back her hair. She hammered the horse through the shallows, water cascading in great silver fountains and reined in beside me.

Her name was a joke, of course, for she was a small hippy girl of twenty-five or so with long, ash-white hair, good breasts and a wide, generous mouth in the calmest of faces.

She sat looking down at me, water trickling between her breasts, quite unconcerned. 'Hello there,' she said. 'What's the score?'

Her English was excellent, but it always tended to have a faintly old-fashioned ring to it. The kind of language used by private detectives in old movies.

I said, 'I'm looking for the Turk.'

'He was here.'

She slid from the horse's back and stood there rubbing her buttocks with both hands. The faint, blonde shadow between her thighs suddenly had me going on all six cylinders in a way I had forgotten was possible. I took out my cigarettes quickly and offered her one.

When I held out a match in my cupped hands they trembled more than somewhat. She held my wrists and looked up at me gravely. 'You're shaking like a tree in a storm, man. What's wrong with you? Do you fancy me, is that it?'

'You're damn right I do.'

'Then let's get to it.'

She threw herself down on the towel, one knee raised, still smoking the cigarette. I fought the Devil like a man, took a deep breath and squatted beside her.

'Not today, angel, if your ego can take it.'

95

Still that same complete lack of concern. 'All right,' she said. 'What do you want?'

'The Turk.'

'Like I told you, he was here, but he's gone now.'

'He couldn't have stayed long.'

'Didn't need to. He had the black mood on him. When he gets that way all he needs is a little comfort and he comes running to moma.' She put her hands between her legs. 'I've got just what the doctor ordered right here. The one sure thing that pulls the Turk back from the edge of the cliffs every time.'

For a moment I forgot why I was there. I leaned forward, utterly fascinated and said urgently, 'What is it, Bertha? What is it that's killing him a little bit more each day.'

'That's easy, man,' she said calmly. 'He's a murderer, isn't he?'

It rocked me back on my heels like a stiff slap across the face. I said slowly, 'What in the hell are you talking about?'

She sat up and stubbed her cigarette out in the sand. 'But you're his best friend, aren't you? Didn't he ever tell you what happened back there in Nam?'

'All right,' I said. 'You tell me.'

'In a pig's eye, I will. Let him do his own thing in his own way.' She reached for a palette and half-a-dozen brushes and stood up. 'If you want him he's at the bull fights, or that's what the man said. Now get to hell out of here. I've got work to do.'

She started to paint instantly in a kind of controlled frenzy and I turned away and climbed the path quickly to the farm.

He's a murderer, isn't he? That one phrase rattled around in my head ceaselessly and refused to go away as I drove back to Ibiza.

The corrida started at four o'clock and we were there in good time, for Sister Claire, impatient at the delay, had insisted on coming.

The Plaza de Toros at Ibiza is like bull-rings in most small towns in Spain. A large concrete circle, not particularly elegant to look at, but then the *aficionados* are only interested in what takes place inside the ring anyway.

I got two tickets for the shady side which were naturally more expensive, but it was still hot enough to be uncomfortable in the sun. I also hired a couple of cushions at twenty-five pesetas apiece and we went up the steps and out into the open.

There wasn't too large a crowd which was what I'd been counting on. For one thing the tourist season hadn't really started and for another, the bill was nothing much. Average bulls and run-of-the-mill toreros.

I settled Sister Claire in a good place then started to work my way round the plaza, just above the barrera. I was wasting my time and arrived back at my starting point as the small band struck up a gay march.

'Any sign of him?' she asked.

I shook my head. 'Don't worry. There's still time. It's a three-hour programme.'

Just then the President of the Plaza arrived with his entourage and took his place to a scattering of applause from the crowd. The little band broke into *La Virgin de la Macarena*, that most loved of all *paso dobles* played at the bull festivals, music that seemed to put a knife in the heart of everyone who heard it.

Death waits, it seemed to say, down there in the arena at four o'clock in the afternoon and then the gate opened and the procession started in, three matadors first in line, brave in their embroidered capes and suits, peons and cuadrillas behind them followed by the picadors on horseback.

There was a positive blaze of colour down there in the ring, the crowd applauded, the procession scattered and the toreros handed their embroidered capes to those favoured in the crowd. Then they took up their plain fighting capes and there was something of a hiatus.

'What is everyone waiting for?' Sister Claire demanded.

'The signal from the President to begin,' I said. 'Do you see that door across the ring?'

'The red door?'

I nodded. 'Toreros call it the Gate of Fear. You'll see why in a moment.'

A bugle sounded high and clear, there was a sudden silence and then that red door creaked open.

The bull came out of the darkness like a runaway train, gaily-coloured ribbons fluttering behind him. As he skidded to a halt, the crowd roared and the peons moved out to meet him, capes ready to try him out for the torero.

At the same moment there was a sudden high-pitched cry and I looked over to my right in time to see Turk poised on top of the concrete wall surrounding the ring.

He yelled, 'Heh, bull baby, to hell with those bastards. What about me?'

Then he jumped out over the barrera into the ring, the tails of his headband fluttering out behind him, landing in the sand on his hands and knees.

It was just the kind of thing the crowd loved. They started to applaud and then with a cry of alarm that might have come from a single mighty throat, every man in the plaza was on his feet as the Turk ran forward, flung himself on his knees a few yards in front of the bull and bared his chest.

'Come on, bull baby,' he cried. 'The Pass of Death, just for me. Once is all it takes.'

The bull charged him, head-down and one

of the toreros, probably moving faster than he'd ever done in his life before, got the cape out just in time and pulled the bull to one side.

And that was very much that because a moment later four large policemen arrived on the run and grabbing a limb apiece, dragged him out of the limelight, kicking and struggling.

The crowd booed or cheered as the mood took it, the air was full of catcalls. The bugle blew three times to restore order and Sister Claire tugged at my sleeve.

I nodded, 'That's right, Sister. That was Harry Turkovich.'

We were in the waiting room at police headquarters in the Avenida Ignacio Wallis for a good hour after I'd sent my message in to Lieutenant Cordoba. The desk sergeant knew me well for I had been there on the same errand many times, but he had never given me coffee before and that little courtesy, I knew, aimed entirely at Sister Claire.

'Will they let him go?' she whispered to

me at one point. I nodded. 'Oh, yes, there's not much doubt of that.'

'How can you be so sure?'

'Last October there was a force ten gale in this area – near hurricane proportions and it caused a lot of damage in the harbour. A fishing boat turned turtle by the breakwater with five men and a boy trapped inside the hull – all locals. Turk brought them out one by one, in spite of those terrible seas. Made over twenty dives. The cuts in various parts of his body needed better than forty stitches.'

'I see,' she said. 'In Ibiza, he's something of a hero?'

'No, I think it's deeper than that,' I said. 'They respect courage, but Turk had something more to offer than mere physical bravery. He kept on trying in spite of the number of times he was beaten back. He showed them he was willing to die rather than give up. An honourable concept and one Spaniards particularly would appreciate.'

'A strange man,' she said. 'You and he must be great friends, I think.'

I nodded. 'But different.'

'In what way?'

I thought about it for a moment or so and came up with the perfect answer. 'The real difference between the Turk and me is that at close quarters, with his finger on the trigger, he thinks about it.'

'And you?'

'Not for one split second.'

There was a kind of instant pain in her eyes, but before she could say anything, Lieutenant Cordoba came in. He was a tall, rather scholarly-looking man in a crumpled uniform with an expression of settled melancholy on his face as if perpetually distressed at the evil to be found in his fellow men. And yet, among what criminal class there was on the island, he was more feared than any other police officer.

He saluted Sister Claire courteously then said to me, 'We meet again, Mr Nelson. Always the same. Will he never learn, this friend of yours?'

'He's a sick man,' I said. 'I think you know this.'

'There is a limit to the world's patience; is it not so, Sister?'

Sister Claire said simply, 'But not to God's.'

Cordoba was not in the least put out. 'A point, Sister, a point. However, Mr Nelson, try to keep him out of the bullring in future. He could bring others into harm there, as I think you must agree.'

'I'll do my best.'

'Good, then I'll have him at the main entrance in ten minutes. Please to take him away as quickly as possible.'

He saluted Sister Claire again, the door closed behind him softly.

When Turk appeared in the entrance his face seemed fleshless in the strong evening sun, gaunt from malnutrition and the fact that he hadn't shaved for three days didn't help. He looked like some emaciated saint.

As he came forward, I saw that he was trembling violently and he had to grab hold of the edge of the jeep's canvas tilt to steady himself.

His eyes were burning. He looked from me to Sister Claire and said, 'My God, where did you find it?'

'Claire Bouvier,' I said.

For a moment it almost brought him back to the here and now. 'You mean this is the chick you found running through the pines in the buff last night?' He turned to Sister Claire. 'What a thing to happen to a decent, Catholic girl.'

And then he doubled over with a sudden cry and I got an arm about him quickly. 'What is it, Turk?'

'Jesus, baby, but I need a fix,' he said. 'I need a fix bad. You get me to the boat fast. You hear now?'

It was only a five-minute drive which was a good thing because I don't think he could have taken much more. Breaking local traffic regulations, I drove along the breakwater and braked to a halt right above the *Mary Grant*. He was out of the jeep and down the ladder before I'd switched off the engine.

When I went down below, I found him on his knees in the lavatory, scrabbling frantically behind the pan. He finally produced a tin box and brushed past me into the galley his teeth bared like an animal getting ready to fight or die.

He rolled up his sleeve, exposing an arm pitted with scores of tracks, some of them weeping with infection, and knotted a brown lace around his upper arm in a rough tourniquet to make the veins stand out. Then he filled a small bottle with water from the tap, dropped in a couple of heroin tablets from the tin box, struck a match and held it underneath.

He turned and grinned savagely as Sister Claire arrived, all the agony of life at this level in his eyes. 'It's a great life if you don't weaken, duchess.'

He took a hypodermic from the table drawer and filled it from the bottle then as he attempted to insert the needle, doubled over in pain, dropping it to the floor.

He collapsed into a chair shaking violently and it was Sister Claire who picked up the hypodermic, straightened his arm and ran the needle into a vein expertly. I thought I had got used to most things, but when that filthy, blunted needle went into the Turk, it was as if it went into me also.

He leaned back, eyes closed. Sister Claire said, 'Have you any idea what his daily intake is, Mr Nelson?'

'Seven grains of heroin and six of cocaine last I heard.'

She nodded. 'And one twelfth of a grain of heroin is the normal dose to relieve pain.'

'Exactly.'

A moment later, Turk opened his eyes and smiled, all strain for the moment having left that ravaged face.

'Now then, General,' he said. 'Just exactly what was it you wanted?'

But by then I'd had enough. I said, 'Let her tell you. I'll be back in an hour,' and I plunged wildly through the saloon and went up the companionway.

I've always liked graveyards so I went for a walk in one of the oldest in Europe, the Puig dels Molins as the Ibizans call it. Hill of the Mills. It's actually part of the town, the hillside dotted with olive trees and caper shrubs with prickly pear trees also adding colour to the landscape. There are better than two thousand graves on the hill mainly dating from Phoenician times and the whole area is honeycombed with tombs, many connected by underground galleries.

It suited my mood and I sat on the edge of a stone tomb, smoked a cigarette and looked out over the harbour. The spectacle of Turk had physically sickened me which was strange because I'd seen it all before.

Thinking about it now, I think it was simply some psychological turning point. One thing was certain. I wanted out. I wanted to break right out of the narrow circumference of my life into something different. Something very different and that, as the saying went, would take money.

There was only one course open to me, so much was obvious and considering the implication, I was surprised at just how cheerful I felt as I walked down the hill towards the harbour.

* * *

When I went down the companionway to the saloon I found Turk sitting at the table, a chart spread in front of him, a glass of brandy in one hand. There was no sign of Sister Claire.

'Where is she?' I demanded.

'Gone back to her hotel.' He looked up at me. 'She's mad, you know that, don't you? Stark, staring, bloody mad.'

'That's what I told her.'

'On the other hand, it is a great deal of money.' He straightened the chart with one hand. 'This is a British Admiralty chart of the coastal approaches. Not so accurate on the interior. I used to run cigarettes out of this little fishing port near Cape Djinet last year. I know the area quite well.'

'Are you going?'

'Are you?' he demanded. 'It would need two. The daft bitch insists on going herself, but she obviously won't be much help.'

We sat there in silence looking at each other. A fly droned. I helped myself to a glass of brandy. 'What did she offer you?'

'My expenses and ten thousand dollars when we get back.'

I said, 'And she really expects you to do this kind of work for wages?'

'That's right.'

'My God, I wonder what she'd offer me.'

'We've already discussed that – ten thousand.'

'And the Otter? What did she say about that?'

'Not a thing – it's water under the bridge. She's probably the most single-minded woman I ever did see. All she's interested in is that hospital of hers.'

It was so ludicrous as to be laughable. I said, 'You can't be serious. And you still want to go?'

'As I said, it's a great deal of money.'

'Ten thousand dollars and expenses?'

'That isn't the amount I had in mind.' Which, putting it mildly, was a reasonably interesting remark.

'All right,' I said. 'But there's something you ought to know.'

I told him about Talif and the well. It had no visible effect. He simply shrugged his shoulders and said, 'So they play for keeps. That's only to be expected. I'll say it again. Are you going?'

I suppose that, if I'm honest, I'd been aware for quite some time what my answer would be. I held out my hand silently.

He shook it and said gravely, 'Okay, let's go tell her the good news.'

There was no one at the desk when we went in, but she'd told me her room number earlier and we went straight upstairs. The door was ajar and she was standing in the middle of the room looking very angry indeed, her personal belongings and clothing strewn everywhere.

She turned to face us as we went into the room, 'Damn them, damn them, damn them!' she said bitterly.

'You want to watch that language, Duchess, the Devil's listening,' Turk said and shook his head as he surveyed the carnage. 'Whoever it was, he didn't have much time.'

'The fools,' she said. 'Did they expect me to leave the information they want lying around on a scrap of paper?'

'Never mind,' Turk said. 'We've decided to bring a little sunshine into your lonely life.'

She sat very, very still, staring up at him fixedly. 'You mean you'll go?' she said. 'You'll take me into the Khufra?'

'It must be my day for mental aberrations.'

She turned to look up at me. 'And you, Mr Nelson?'

'He goes, too,' Turk told her cheerfully. 'He's my number one boy.'

I won't say there were actually tears in her eyes, but they were certainly what the woman's magazines would have termed suspiciously wet.

'I just don't know what to say.'

'Then don't say a thing,' I told her. 'Just get packed as quickly as possible. You're leaving.'

'Leaving?' she said. 'I don't understand.'

'You can't stay here, that's obvious,' Turk said. 'They're on to you, aren't they? Next time it'll be you they're after.'

She turned to me, looking strangely uncertain. 'But where can I go?'

'You leave that to us,' I told her. 'But I guarantee you one thing. You'll be in the safest place in Ibiza.'

Which I see now, on reflection, was really asking for it.

5

Action by Night

When Juan took us out on the terrace, Lillie was floating in the centre of the pool on an airbed. She slid into the water and swam to the side with a surprisingly expert crawl stroke.

Turk gave her a hand up and she flung her arms around his neck and kissed him full on the mouth. 'Hello, you gorgeous beast,' she said.

He slapped her backside and helped her into the robe Juan held out. As she tied the belt, she turned to me. 'I'm not sure I ought to speak to you. You promised to come back last night. What happened? Did you decide to shack up with your little friend after all?'

Sister Claire moved out of the shadows at that precise moment. 'Good evening, Miss St Claire,' she said. 'It's nice to see you again.'

Lillie stood there, staring at her for a long, long moment and then astonished us all by laughing harshly, a finger pointing dramatically.

'That's it, of course. The hair.' She turned and grabbed at my arm. 'Didn't I tell you last night there was something about her I couldn't quite place? Something to do with an old movie?'

'That's right,' I said.

'It was a thing I did for Fox. Convent life in the raw. They hacked off my hair in the first reel. The only reason I let them do it was because my agent swore it was going to be the greatest thing since sliced bread. Another Oscar. Needless to say it sank without a trace.'

Juan handed her one of those tall, frosted glasses without which she always seemed partially undressed. She rattled the ice, looking us over in the silence. 'All right, who's going to read me the script?'

'It's simple enough,' I said. 'Sister Claire needs somewhere to stay for a couple of days.'

'You mean somewhere safe presumably, or was last night's little episode just one of those things?'

I glanced at Turk enquiringly and Lillie went on, 'I'd like to know what I'm getting into, that's all or is that too much to ask?'

It was Sister Claire who answered. 'I think Miss St Claire is perfectly right. I personally haven't the least objection to giving her the background to the whole affair.'

'Why don't we just put an ad in the local paper?' I said. 'That way everybody would know.'

'Cool it, lover,' Lillie told me crisply. 'My house and my party, in case you'd forgotten, so why don't you and the Turk clear off like good little boys and leave us womenfolk to have a nice cosy chat.'

'And what exactly would you like us to do?' I asked. 'Jump off the cliff?'

'A possibility – or you could just sit in the garden for half an hour and have a couple of drinks.'

She took Sister Claire in through the window without another word. Turk said, 'She always did make a good exit.'

'Do you think she'll play?'

'Oh, sure. The only excitement she ever gets these days is between the sheets. This little affair will make a change and she's not being asked to do anything very dangerous. Bed and board for a couple of days is all.'

Which made sense so I asked Juan to bring us a couple of gin and tonics and we went out into the garden.

The lower terrace which ended on the very edge of the point was particularly beautiful. There were almond trees and a few date palms and then a low balustrade and beyond it, cliffs fell a good hundred and fifty feet to the narrow fringe of beach below. There was a concrete pier, a speed-boat moored beside it, and an old boathouse.

The sun was still on the horizon, an orange ball suspended in a sky the colour of brass. It was all very beautiful. I sipped the drink Juan brought me and watched the lights of a cruise ship pass a mile out.

116

Turk, however, had other things on his mind than the beauties of nature. He'd brought the Admiralty chart of the Khufra area with him and leaned over it with a pencil and paper, making various calculations.

After a while, he sat back and reached for his drink. 'By my reckoning, we should hit the Algerian coast in twelve hours if we get a clear run.'

'And how long from there to get where we're going?'

'God knows. I asked the duchess for the exact position of the plane, but to be frank with you, she wasn't exactly forthcoming. Said she'd give it to me when we hit the coast and not before.'

'The act of a true Christian.'

'And I can't say I blame her,' Lillie said, moving out of the shadows. 'Not if she's having to do business with a couple of objects like you.'

She was wearing a cheongsam in heavy green silk worked with a scarlet dragon whose forked tongue ran to the tip of each breast. It was buttoned tightly at the neck and split

117

to the thigh on either side which, taken together with the high-heeled gold shoes, made her look uncomfortably like a Saigon whore.

She sat on my knee casually and leaned across the table to look at the chart. 'The whole thing sounds like the worst kind of B picture material. We don't want it good. We want it by next Monday.'

'You should know,' I told her cheerfully.

She ignored me and said to Turk, 'From what she's just told me, this Khufra place sounds like the kind of item the Almighty threw off when he wasn't really trying.'

'You could say that.' Turk tapped his pencil on the chart. 'There's only one navigable way in here at the mouth of the river and that's hedged about with sandbanks that are here one day and gone the next so even the chart's no more than a guideline.'

'And inside?'

'Ten thousand square miles of mud, reeds higher than a man, just to make it that much more difficult to see where you're going, a maze of waterways and lagoons. So many, a guy could spend his life going round in circles without getting anywhere.'

'Or looking for that plane.'

'Only we know where we're going,' Turk said.

She corrected him instantly. 'You mean Sister Claire does.'

'All right, but we still know more than this Taleb guy.' He drew a circle round Zarza which was marked on the map as being about fifteen miles inland. 'That's the village Talif took the girl to after the crash so the plane can't be too far from there.'

Lillie turned and looked at me over her shoulder. 'This guy Talif – what about him?'

'Search me,' I said.

She frowned slightly, then turned to Turk who shrugged. 'Maybe he just got scared and decided he'd be better off making a run for the hills with the money she gave him.'

She looked at me again, searchingly, obviously unhappy about the whole thing, but before she could make any comment Sister Claire appeared, escorted by Juan.

Lillie said, 'There you are, honey. We've

just been looking things over. Not that it makes any difference, but I think these boys are crazy. I've just been telling them so.'

'You must excuse me if I fail to agree with that opinion,' Sister Claire said, and she smiled at both of us. 'I think they are magnificent.'

'So do we,' Turk said, standing up.

'Aren't you two staying for dinner?' Lillie demanded.

Turk didn't give me a chance to reply. 'No, we've got work to do.'

Sister Claire put a hand on his arm and he turned to her. 'And when do we leave, Mr Turkovich?'

'Turk, Duchess, Turk. How many times do I have to tell you?' He folded the chart. 'When we leave depends entirely on how much Jack and I can get done tonight. I'd say sometime tomorrow afternoon. The main thing is to hit the Algerian coast after dark.'

Her smile deepened, became positively radiant. She said, 'Oh, bless you, dear friend. And you, Mr Nelson.' Which was all suddenly rather embarrassing, especially with Lillie in the background leering over the top of her glass.

I said to Turk, 'All right, we'd better get moving. We'll see you tomorrow morning, Sister.'

As we walked away through the garden Lillie called, 'I'll see you to the door, boys. Back in a minute, honey.'

We waited for her, but when she caught up with us she said, 'So you're working for wages, are you?'

We both turned. Turk said, 'That's it, oh love of my life.'

'Bastards!' she said and closed the door.

There didn't seem to be very much to say after that so we got in the jeep and drove away.

We stopped at Tijola first to get the diving equipment we'd used that morning. Turk suggested a drink at the beach bar before going up to the cottage and I agreed because I wanted a word with him anyway.

A couple of local fishermen sat on high

stools talking to the owner. I ordered brandies and coffee and we went and sat at a table as far away from them as possible. It was very quiet, the only sound the cicadas and the surf creaming in.

Turk said, 'Okay, General, get it off your chest.'

'All right,' I said, 'how much – the whole pot?'

'What in the hell do you take me for? A thief?' He managed to sound genuinely injured. 'No, the way I see it, if everything works out okay and we exit in one piece, I reckon that earns us fifty per cent of the take. I can't see anything unreasonable about that. How about you?'

'What I think doesn't count. I can't imagine Sister Claire sitting still for it.'

'It's a hell of a sight better than a hundred per cent of nothing.'

The barman brought our brandy and coffee. I sat for a while in silence staring into the night thinking about it.

'For God's sake, General, if you think you owe her something, think again. You lost

your plane as a direct result of helping her –
right? Does she suggest a little compensation
maybe? Does she hell.'

He tossed back his brandy and reached for
mine. I said, 'All she can think of is that
hospital she wants to build back in Dacca.'

'Which they'll promptly blow up again the
next year's war.' I was surprised at the
savagery in his voice. The anger. 'Okay, so
she wants to do good, she can do it on half
rations. Anything we get, we earn. It isn't
going to be any picnic going in there. Don't
you kid yourself.'

'I'm not.' I pushed back my chair. 'Not
about a single damn thing. Come up to the
cottage when you're ready.'

I got into the jeep and drove along the
edge of the beach slowly. What he had said
was perfectly true, and Sister Claire was
certainly being infuriatingly unreasonable
about the whole affair. Why then should I
feel so disturbed about it all?

I couldn't get it out of my mind. Was still
thinking about it when I opened the door
and went into the living room. It was quite

dark, of course, so I reached for a match to light the oil lamp and when it flared into life, I found a man sitting on the edge of the bed waiting for me.

I lit the lamp, then turned to face him. He wore a panama hat, white linen suit and his hands were folded across the head of a silver mounted ebony walking stick. The eyes, which contrasted strangely with the brown skin, were very bright blue, but that, of course, would be a legacy from his French mother.

I said, 'Don't tell me, let me guess.'

'Pierre Taleb at your service, Mr Nelson. I thought it was time we had a little chat.'

'Colonel Pierre Taleb of the Algerian Security Police. Let's get it right.'

'Exactly.'

'I wonder what the Spanish police would have to say about you or do they know you're here?'

'I have always found them most cooperative.'

'I see,' I said. 'And how do they feel about bodies in wells?' I went across to the cupboard, took out a bottle of brandy and poured myself a small one, mainly for something to do more than anything else.

He said, 'Mr Nelson, let's come directly to the point. The Bouvier woman has certain information I want. You understand me?'

I've always been a bad liar, but I tried, 'I don't know what in the hell you're talking about.'

'Excellent,' he said. 'I see I have not been mistaken in you. Claire Bouvier believes that the contents of the plane in which she crashed into the Khufra Marshes seven years ago are hers to dispose of as she wills.'

'That seems reasonable enough to me.'

'You are wrong, Mr Nelson. Whatever is in that plane is the property of the government and people of Algeria. You understand me? It can't be any other way.'

'Then why in the hell don't you go and salvage it?'

'Where would one begin, Mr Nelson? Ten thousand square miles of swamp.' He shook his head and sighed, 'A strange business. We had thought them all dead until this wretched man Talif was spotted in Marseilles.'

There was silence for a while, I tried the brandy. It tasted foul but I poured some more anyway. 'All right, what do you want with me?'

'Simple,' he said. 'You get the position of the plane out of her. I'm sure she trusts you to the hilt by now.'

'And in return?'

'Ten thousand dollars. American. Payable by draft on a Geneva bank.'

'And my plane?' I said. 'What about the Otter?'

'Yes, that really was most regrettable.' He sighed. 'I'm afraid I had to use what you might term local labour and it got a little out of hand. But you have a point. Let me see, now? Would another five thousand square the situation?' He held out his hand. 'Agreed?'

I said, 'Nothing doing.'

He said patiently, 'Mr Nelson, the French squeezed us dry for years. Squeezed us until there was nothing left. But now we are free

126

and what is ours, we hold. Now then, I will ask you again . . .'

'Why don't you get stuffed?' I suggested.

'Ah, yes.' He sighed again. 'One of your more inelegant English phrases. I see now that I was mistaken in you.'

He snapped his fingers and the Terrible Twins came in from the kitchen.

The first time I'd seen them they'd seemed like something out of a nightmare, but not now. Now they were too close to be anything but real and the stench was appalling. With their filthy matted hair and beards, the tattered clothes, they really did look something less than human, especially the one who had walked into the jeep door. His right eye was closed and that side of his face was disfigured by a green-black bruise.

I said to Taleb, 'Where in the hell did you find these two, for God's sake? The town sewer?'

A quiet voice said, 'They came with me, man. They're my friends.'

I didn't bother turning, simply lashed out backwards with my left heel, connecting satisfactorily with a shin then I vaulted over the bed and turned to face them, back to the wall.

Redshirt was down on one knee clutching his right shin, his face twisted in pain. And the eyes behind the wire spectacles were filled with tears.

'Shit, man,' he said in that surprisingly soft voice of his, 'what for you got to do a thing like that? We're going to have to teach you a lesson now. Isn't that so, boys?'

The Terrible Twins howled like great apes. One of them actually beat his chest with both fists, then they charged. I threw the bed clothes at them, then turned the bed over. One of them went sprawling, bringing the other down with him and I vaulted across and ran for the kitchen door.

I'd have made it, too, if it hadn't been for Taleb, who got his stick between my legs at exactly the wrong moment. I went down like a stone falling and the next moment they were swarming all over me.

It was nothing like as bad as I might have

reasonably expected in the circumstances, which didn't make the future look any too bright. They lashed my wrists behind me and the stink of them at close quarters was really quite something.

They finally dragged me to my feet, supporting me between them. Taleb took a step towards me and Redshirt shoved him to one side. 'Not now, man. Later.'

I stood there waiting for it, unable to move a limb, so tightly was I held by the Terrible Twins. Redshirt took off his spectacles, cleaned them meticulously with the tail of his shirt.

'My friends call me Geronimo,' he said. 'You know why that is, man?'

'Don't tell me, let me guess,' I said. 'Your breath smells.' He sighed heavily and adjusted the wire spectacles. 'Wrong again, man. It's because I'm cruel – cruel by nature. Just can't seem to help myself. There's a name for it only I can never remember what it is.'

'Why not try psychopath?' I suggested helpfully.

He seemed delighted. 'That's it, man. That's

exactly it.' Then he hit me in the stomach with his clenched fist.

I went down on my knees. The great, round, brass buckle on his belt, suddenly at eye level, seemed to swell to enormous proportions. Then it started to spin, dwindling into a tiny golden eye.

I was aware of being carted from the house, the sound of the surf, of being thrown into the bottom of an inflatable dinghy, but most of this was confused.

I was just about back to normal when we bumped against the hull of some larger craft and when I was pulled upright, I found myself looking over the rail to the deck of a broken-down old launch, all peeling paint, rust and mildew. God alone knows where they'd got it from. It was obviously somebody's working boat because it stank of fish and the deck-house was festooned with nets stretched out to dry.

Geronimo and Taleb were already on deck and the Twins followed, dragging me between them. In the sickly yellow glow of the deck light Geronimo resembled one of those waxwork figures in the Chamber of Horrors that look ready to spring into life at any moment.

Taleb looked distinctly worried. He cleared his throat to speak and Geronimo said, 'Not now, man. You can have what's left.'

He nodded briefly and to my amazement one of the Twins untied my hands. Then they grabbed a wrist each and pulled me flat on my back.

'Tie his wrists to the rails,' Geronimo ordered.

At the same time he produced a spring blade gutting knife from his pocket. When he pressed the button, the blade jumped out with a sharp click like a snake striking. He smiled gently and squatted beside me.

'You've got a lot of the right stuff in you, man, I'll give you that, but this is where you get cut down to size.'

Two things happened then in quick succession. First, Taleb produced a revolver from his inside pocket, cocking it in the same motion. 'I think we are forgetting who is in charge here,' he said softly.

Geronimo turned to look up at him, then with a quick, violent motion, he drove the point of the knife into the deck. 'Are you going to give me trouble, man?'

At the same moment, a dark shadow came up out of the water behind them and slipped under the rail. 'Is this a private fight?' Turk said, 'Or can anyone join in?'

A long-handled gaff stood against the deck-house and it was already in his hands as Taleb wheeled round. The gaff moved upwards in a quick arc, the revolver clattered to the deck.

The Twins' grip had already slackened and I pulled my right hand free, punched the nearest jaw and kicked out at Geronimo. For a moment, all was confusion. One of the Twins flung himself at Turk, who gave him the butt of the gaff in the belly.

'Over you go, General,' he shouted.

I cleared the rail, head-down, in what was hardly an Olympic style dive, but good enough in the circumstances. The water was ice-cold, or perhaps it only felt that way.

In any event, it revived me wonderfully. I surfaced several yards from the boat and found Turk close beside me, laughing like a crazy man.

We swam for the shore side by side. Behind us, all was confusion on deck. As my feet touched bottom, an engine broke into life and when I turned, knee-deep in water, the old fishing boat was moving out to sea.

Turk stood up beside me, still laughing. 'We live, General, we certainly live,' he said. 'You've got to admit that.'

We drove into Ibiza to the *Mary Grant* with the rest of the diving gear. When we went into the saloon, Turk dumped the aqualung he was carrying, got down on his hands and knees and opened a cupboard under a bench.

I expected to see him produce another of his eternal bottles. Instead, he felt inside and took out what proved to be a false floor. He turned and handed me a Browning automatic pistol.

'Loaded for bear, General,' he said.

'From now on I'd say it would be better to be safe than sorry.'

He took another out for himself and squatted there on the floor, checking the clip.

I said, 'Where in the hell did you get these?'

'A friend of a friend.' He grinned. 'This is nothing.'

He turned to his hidey hole again and took out a couple of Sterling submachine guns and a large tin box marked WD which could only mean it was British Army Ordnance.

He put the box on the table, opened it and produced various items. 'Plastic gelignite – R14. Works well underwater. Two dozen chemical fuses. All the comforts of home.'

I pushed the Browning into my belt and examined one of the fuses gingerly. 'They really work these things?'

'Like a charm. If there's any blasting to be done when we find that plane, this is the gear to do it.'

'You think it's likely?'

'God knows. You never know with impact damage. She must have gone down hard, that's for certain.'

He put the tin box and the submachine guns back in the hole, replaced the false floor and closed the cupboard.

'Okay, General,' he said as he stood up. 'As you limeys are fond of saying, let's get cracking. We've got work to do.'

The *Mary Grant* was powered by Penta petrol engines so we crossed to the inner harbour and refuelled, then we moved to a mooring close to the place where you get the Formentera boat and Turk got the man he bought his compressed air from to open up.

There were the aqualungs to check, extra air bottles to stow away and the freshwater tank was almost empty. By the time we had seen to all these things and moved back to the usual berth on the breakwater, a couple of hours had gone by.

As we eased in, I stood by the rail with a line ready to tie up. Someone was standing at the top of the ladder. Turk saw him too and immediately swivelled the spotlight mounted on the outside of the wheelhouse to pull him out of the night.

'Senor Turk, is that you?'

It was one of the waiters from the bar we habitually used at the end of the breakwater. I suppose I knew it was trouble straightaway. I tied up quickly and went up the ladder, Turk at my heels.

'Ah, Senor Nelson,' the man said, 'you also. The senorita said either of you would do, but it was most urgent.'

'Which senorita?' Turk demanded.

'The lady from the Villa Rose. Senorita St Claire. She said you were to phone her at once, but that was an hour ago. I came several times. You were not here.'

He said something else also, but we didn't hear him for we were already running along the breakwater. The bar was as crowded as it usually was at that time of night and thick with cigarette smoke. Someone was already on the phone and I waited impatiently. Turk moved to the bar for a drink, I supposed, but when he turned I saw that he had only bought a packet of cigarettes.

He gave me one. They were the local variety, cheap and rough – the kind that took a bite at your throat on the way down. There was a burst of clapping and a guitarist moved in through a bead curtain. Someone passed him a chair. He sat down and started to play a slow, sad, Andalusian melody with something of the night in it.

A moment later a very beautiful girl came through the curtain dressed like a man in high boots, tight pants, frilled shirt and Cordoban hat. She started to dance, almost imperceptibly at first. The world turned in slow motion. At the same moment the man on the phone moved away.

I waited impatiently to the slow burr-burr at the other end, Turk with his head close to mine to hear what was said. It seemed to go on forever and then, with a sharp click, the receiver was lifted and Lillie spoke.

'Villa Rose.'

'Lillie? It's Jack. What's the trouble?'

'You'd better get here fast, lover,' she said. 'They've got your girl friend.'

6

The Children of Light

When we drove up to the gate and I sounded the horn, old Jose appeared as usual with the Alsatian on its chain, which didn't seem to make much sense.

He opened the gate and I drove up the drive quickly and braked to a halt. As we got out of the jeep, the front door opened and Carlo appeared. He was wearing a rather dramatic-looking white bandage and his right eye looked puffy.

Turk said, 'What happened to you, for Christ's sake?'

Carlo didn't say a word, simply turned and led the way inside. The main salon was something of a shambles. A couple of vases and a glass table had been smashed and a curtain ripped down from the French windows and a table was still overturned.

'My God, who did you have in here, the Viet Cong?' Turk demanded.

A door opened and as we turned, Lillie appeared on the landing above. 'I haven't seen anything like it since I last did a barroom brawl on Stage 6 at Metro,' she said, as she came down the stairs.

She wore black and gold silk lounging pyjamas and what looked like at least twenty feet of gold chiffon floated behind her like ectoplasm.

'What happened?' I said.

She snapped a finger and Carlo fitted a Turkish cigarette into a holder and handed it to her. 'We were sitting in here, the good sister and I, having something of a heart-to-heart as women do, when these three quite appalling creatures simply burst in through the French windows.

'Any idea who they were?' Turk asked her, a superfluous question if ever there was one.

'Hippies, darling, and as nasty a threesome

as I've ever seen. The one who seemed to be in charge wore a red shirt, spectacles, long hair – all the usual gear. His two friends were the end. When I was a kid, I worked with a carnival for a while. We had some poor nut who lived in a cage and was billed as The Wild Man of Borneo. He wasn't even in their league.' She made a face. 'God, I can still smell them.'

'So they took Sister Claire?' I said.

She nodded and held out her other hand for the Martini Carlo passed to her. 'I nearly got raped, lover – right there in front of the fire.' She pointed dramatically. 'God alone knows what would have happened if Carlo hadn't arrived when he did.' She turned and raised her glass to him. 'He fought like a tiger, didn't you, darling? Put all three of them to flight.'

'Only he couldn't manage to stop them taking Sister Claire with them?' Turk said, with some irony.

'He was thinking of me, darling, weren't you, Carlo?' She went and patted his face. 'He saved my . . .' here she hesitated and went on '. . . my life.'

Carlo kissed the palm of her hand, eyes

burning. I think she'd almost said he'd saved her virginity, but that would have been too much, even for Lillie.

I said, 'So much for your bloody Alsatian.'

'But they didn't come the front way, lover,' she said. 'That's the whole point. They came by boat. After they'd left I ran to the point and saw them going down the cliff path to the beach. There was a boat at the jetty. Someone was waiting for them!'

'How can you be certain?'

'The deck light was on. I saw him quite clearly. After all, it's not far. He wore a panama and a white suit. Didn't look their type at all.'

So that was very much that. I turned to Turk who shrugged. 'Now what do we do?'

'God knows,' I said. 'But we've got to make some kind of move. The thought of her in the hands of these creeps isn't anything that I could live with.'

'Of course, I could have called the police,' Lillie said. 'But I didn't think you'd want that. I mean, it would put the lid on your whole deal, wouldn't it?'

'Without her there isn't any deal,' I said.

'Then you'd better start looking, lover,' she said. 'But fast. I shouldn't think there'd be much left to bury after those pigs have had their way.'

Which was a point. I could only hope that Taleb had learned his lesson and was back in control, gun in hand.

The Turk had walked to the bar in the corner to help himself to a drink. Now, he turned with an oath and tossed his glass on to the fireplace.

'Big Bertha,' he said.

'Now look, darling,' Lillie told him. 'I've definitely had enough for one night. I just couldn't take any more.'

Which quite simply wasn't true for, if I knew my Lillie, she'd loved every golden moment.

I said to Turk, 'What about Big Bertha?'

'She knows every hippie on the island, doesn't she? If anyone can give us a line on this Geronimo creep, she can.'

He was already on his way to the door. I said to Lillie, 'Can we bring her back here?'

143

'Why not,' she said. 'If there's anything to bring. It should be an interesting story.'

She turned and held out her empty glass to Carlo and I went after Turk fast.

Bertha was at home, which was something. We could see a light in her window for at least a mile along the dreadful road.

The door stood open to the night and when I switched off the engine she called, 'Come on in, whoever you are.'

She was standing at the easel, barefooted as usual, but wearing an ankle-length kaftan worked with wooden beads.

She said without looking round, 'Sit down, why don't you? Take the weight off.'

Turk slapped her firm buttocks. 'Sorry, angel, we don't have the time.'

She turned round in surprise, then flung down the palette and brush in disgust. 'Not you two,' she groaned. 'Will you kindly get the hell out of here? I'm not in the mood for it team handed tonight.'

'That's all right, sweetie,' Turk told her

soothingly. 'We're not after your virginity – just information. Have you ever heard of a creep called Geronimo?'

'Red shirt, wire glasses,' I said, 'and the hair-do to go with them.'

She looked at me for a long, cool moment, then snapped a finger at the Turk who took out his cigarettes and gave her one.

'Okay,' she said. 'And what's the bum been up to this time?' Then she coughed suddenly, looked first at the cigarette, then at Turk. 'What's got into you? This is tobacco.'

I said, 'He snatched a friend of ours earlier tonight along with a couple of left-overs from the Stone Age.'

'Castor and Pollux,' she said.

At any other time it could have seemed funny, but I didn't feel much like laughing.

Turk said, 'You know where we might find them?'

'This friend of yours who was snatched,' she said. 'Was it a chick?'

'You could say that, but not for himself. They were on wages.'

'Still bad.' She shook her head. 'Those guys

are straight out of page ten in the horror comics. I mean, they're so bent, it's not true.'

'Can you help us,' I demanded.

'Why should I?'

I didn't know what to say and it was Turk who answered for me. 'Okay, angel, so you're the original hard apple who doesn't give a monkey's end for anyone. Try this for size. The girl they've got their paws on is a nun.'

She didn't exactly cross herself, but she didn't like it, I could see that straightaway. She flipped her cigarette out through the window and said crisply, 'I can tell you where Geronimo will be at ten o'clock tonight for certain, if that's any good, or Harvey Grauber, a rose by any other name stinking just as badly. He's a leading man with a little stock company that call themselves the Children of Light.'

'What are they? A hippie commune?'

She nodded. 'Something like that. They've been squatting in and around an old farmhouse near Halva for four or five months now.'

'And how can you be so certain where this Harvey cat will be at ten?' the Turk demanded.

'Because it's his turn, man,' Bertha said. 'Cut off his legs and he'd make it on his stumps before he'd miss that. Ever heard of the Seed King?'

Turk looked at me blankly. I said, 'Ancient Greece, way, way back. They used to choose a young man every year to be the favoured one. For a year, everything he wanted, wine, women – you name it. There was an unfortunate pay-off. They used to tear him to pieces and soak the newly ploughed earth with his blood.'

'Don't tell me, let me guess,' Turk said. 'They thought it was good for the crops.'

Bertha ignored him and stayed with me. 'The Children of Light are on the same kick minus the blood in the furrows bit. They vary the bill once a month and the lucky man only gets to the chicks on his first night.'

'You'll have to come again on that one,' Turk said.

'I mean, if you take Harvey for example, he's head man for a month, but he only gets one big night with the girls.'

'And that's tonight?'

'At ten sharp,' she said. 'Quite a gig. They once had a guy who was reputed to have laid eighteen, but they tell me he needed an oxygen tent and a doctor afterwards.'

'Okay,' Turk said. 'Will you tell us how to get to this place?'

'I'll do better than that. I'll show you the way. I wouldn't miss seeing Harvey get his for anything.'

The farmhouse at Halva was about three miles inland from the coast near Escubells, a wild, rather lonely spot high in the Sierra de San Jose. We approached along a winding cart track which followed the contours of the hills closely, dark, sterile valleys dropping away to the right of us in the light of the moon.

We pulled into a stand of pine trees at Bertha's suggestion and continued on foot, cutting directly across the hillside, climbing the ancient terraces like giant steps.

I could hear singing faintly in the distance and it grew louder, quite suddenly, when we went over the ridge and looked down into a small valley and saw the farmhouse in the centre of a clump of pine trees below.

A large fire was burning in the yard and perhaps two dozen people squatted around it in a circle. When we got really close it became apparent that they were working themselves up into a frenzy over one of those Indian temple dirges on the lines of Hari Krishna.

We crouched in the shelter of the trees maybe twenty yards beyond the campfire. There were sixteen girls and eight men, I counted.

As if reading my thoughts, Bertha whispered, 'Do you know anything about the Law of Diminishing Returns?'

'Basic economics, isn't it?'

'Harvey-boy is certainly going to see it in practice tonight.'

The Children of Light all looked depressingly alike for individualists who had cut themselves adrift from society rather than surrender their selfhood. Everybody seemed to have the same Jesus hair do and headband.

Some of the men wore moustaches, but otherwise, the only real difference between the sexes was that the men wore shorter kaftans than the women.

Somebody started to beat a hand drum. There was silence. A few words followed from one of the women, hands held up to the moon. Everybody started chanting, swaying from side-to-side and someone moved out of the farmhouse escorted by two women.

It was Geronimo or Harvey, depending on what you wanted to call him. He was wearing his headband and a long, white robe. The moonlight glinted on his wire glasses beautifully.

Turk said softly, 'What does he do? Pull it up or take it off?'

Bertha said, 'The real business of the evening starts any time now. I'll go down and get as near to the head of the queue as I can. We'll take it from there.'

'You sure they'll let you join?' Turk asked her.

'Meet a founder member of the Order,' she

said and moved away through the shadows quickly.

We got in through the rear of the old farmhouse easily enough and found ourselves in what was obviously the kitchen. The door stood ajar and a considerable amount of grunting and groaning sounded from the living room.

I peered round the edge of the door and discovered Harvey working away manfully in the light of a small paraffin lamp. Not being a voyeur in any sense of the word, I withdrew hastily. Turk took a quick look, then produced his cigarettes and offered me one.

'Disgusting, I don't know what the world's coming to.'

'They were doing it in caves,' I said. 'Nothing changes.'

Harvey's partner moved on. There was a pause, then the outside door opened again. As I peered round, Bertha entered.

Harvey closed in on her fast. She held him tight, as Turk and I slipped into the room, then said softly, 'You're facing the wrong way, sweetie.'

As she twisted him round, Turk put a fist in his stomach, a knee in the descending face that splintered the glasses and ducked to catch him across the left shoulder.

He turned and hurried out with his burden. I said to Bertha, 'Will you be all right?'

'Sure, you get to hell out of here. I'll stay and entertain the girls.' She laughed suddenly. 'Heh, come to think of it, this could be quite a gig.'

As I turned to leave, she blew out the lamp.

We dumped Harvey in the back of the jeep and drove back down the track, taking a side turning just before the Escubells road that finally brought us out on a lonely hillside at the edge of high cliffs above the sea.

There was a dried-out, old thorn tree all on its own, branches sticking every which way like withered claws. When Harvey finally came back to life he found himself leaning against it, wrists tied.

He raised his head and stared first at Turk, then at me, the same old malevolence in his eyes, clear in the moonlight. 'You're dead men – both of you.'

Turk laughed softly. 'You've been seeing too many movies, friend. Now I'm going to ask you once and once only, then I get very nasty indeed. Where did you take Sister Claire.'

'In a pig's eye, I'll tell you,' Harvey said venomously. 'And by now, I hope the boys have screwed her good.'

'Naughty, Harvey. Very naughty.'

Turk walked to the jeep and came back with a coil of rope. He quickly knotted one end about Harvey's ankles then tossed the other over a branch of the thorn tree some seven or eight feet above the ground.

'Give me a hand here, General,' he called.

We heaved on the line until Harvey was swinging, head-down, a couple of feet above the ground. Turk quickly tied the free end around the trunk, then he collected a few thorn branches and placed them under Harvey's head.

'You comfortable, Harvey?' he demanded. Harvey tried to kick and only succeeded in swinging. 'What are you going to do, man?' he cried wildly. 'Are you crazy or something?'

'They call you Geronimo,' Turk said, 'and Geronimo was an Apache. Do you know much about them? Probably the finest warriors who ever sat on a horse and the cruellest. I was raised in Arizona and my old grandpappy told me a lot about their little ways. This was one of their favourite turns.' Here, he struck a match and put it to the dried thorns which flared instantly. 'Roast a man nice and slow till his brains swell and burst and run out of his eyeballs.'

'Dear God, no!' It was a howl of agony and Harvey kicked wildly as his hair started to singe.

'All right, I'll ask you for the last time. After this, you burn. Where is she?'

'There's an old warehouse at Punta Gros just this side of Ibiza. They used to load grain there. The boats could come right in. It's deep water.'

'And Sister Claire – she's there?'

'That's right. On my mother's grave.'

154

'You never had a mother.' Turk struck another match and Harvey screamed like a woman. 'It's the truth. I left her there with this guy Taleb. They're in the manager's old office on the second floor facing the sea.'

'And your two chums are there too?'

'That's right.'

'Was she still in one piece when you left?' I demanded.

'Definitely. Nobody laid a glove on her.'

Turk shook his head. 'I don't believe you. Those two creeps couldn't keep their hands off themselves, never mind a woman.'

He lit another match very deliberately and dropped it among the thorns. Harvey said desperately, 'No, listen to me. Taleb gave her till midnight to tell him what he wanted to know. If she doesn't come clean, the boys get her.'

It was too nasty not to be true. Turk said softly, 'You dirty pig,' then he spat in Harvey's face.

Harvey started to blubber like a kid. Turk took out a clasp knife and cut him down. He landed rather painfully on his head and shoulders, scattering the fire, and lay there moaning.

Turk sliced through the rope which secured his wrists and Harvey sat up slowly. He glanced at me fearfully then back to Turk. 'I can go now?'

'Sure you can.' Turk produced the Browning automatic from his waistband and cocked it. 'You can get on your feet and start running just as fast as you can.' Here he gestured towards the edge of the cliff. 'See that white stone. There's a path starts there, goes all the way down to the beach. If I can still see you when I reach the count of three, I'll put a bullet in your head.'

Harvey went away like a dog from the starting gate, head down. He was already at the white stone and past it as Turk called two. Then he disappeared rather abruptly, there was a final cry like a dying fall, then silence.

When I reached the edge of the cliff by the white stone and peered over, there was a sheer drop of two hundred feet to the beach below. Not even a mountain goat could have got down there in one piece.

I turned to Turk. 'No path.'

'I know. I'm a terrible liar.'

He turned and walked back to the jeep.

The old grain warehouse at Punta Gros hadn't been used in years. As Harvey had said, it had been built on the edge of a deep-water inlet so that ocean-going ships could take on their cargo direct from the chutes.

I parked the jeep in among the pine trees about a hundred yards away and went in on foot. There was a faint light at a top floor window, nothing at all below. The front door was locked and refused to open. I tried kicking it, but no one came so I found a brick, smashed in a window next to it and slipped the catch.

I stood in the darkness for a second after scrambling over the sill, just listening, but there wasn't a sound so I decided to make the first move.

'Heh, Taleb, I know you're there,' I called. 'This is Nelson.'

There was a faint scraping sound, perhaps

a foot, I couldn't be certain, somewhere in the gallery of the central hall, high above me.

Taleb called softly, 'What do you want?'

'A deal.'

I waited, listening to the soft footsteps descending the stairs. Suddenly an electric torch was switched on, full in my face.

Taleb said, 'If you make any kind of wrong move I'll kill you. Raise your hands.'

'For God's sake, be your age,' I said. 'Just to show I'm on the level, there's a gun in my left pocket.'

He circled me warily, then moved in from behind and took the Browning. He stepped back, apparently satisfied. 'How did you know where I was.'

'Your pal in the red shirt. Geronimo or Harvey or whatever they call him. I put the screws in him till he told me what I wanted to know.'

'All right. You're here. So what?'

'I want in. I want to join you. Okay, I thought I could do all right on my own, but I know better now.'

There was a short silence, then he said, 'Who needs you, my friend. I have the girl.'

'I know,' I said. 'Harvey told me. If she doesn't cough by midnight, you let those two zombies have their way with her and a fat lot of good that will do you. She won't talk on those terms, not in a million years. She's been trained for that sort of martyrdom.'

And I had touched him, knew it instantly. He said, 'And what would you suggest?'

'She won't talk to save herself, but she will to save me. She couldn't stand by and see me under sentence of death because she refused to open her mouth – get it?'

Taleb laughed softly. 'I certainly do, my friend. I certainly do.'

'Am I in then?' I demanded.

'But of course.' He slipped his revolver inside his coat and patted me on the shoulder. 'I think we may take that for granted.'

I held out my hand, 'Then presumably I can have my gun back.'

He had been holding the Browning in his left hand at arm's length. He raised it now and looked at it in a vaguely abstracted way as if surprised to find he'd got it and then smiled. He extracted the magazine and handed the Browning to me, butt first.

'Many thanks.' I slipped it into my pocket. 'Nothing like mutual trust.'

'But of course.'

We went up a couple of flights of steep concrete steps, Taleb leading the way, perhaps to show me I was wanted after all. There was a narrow iron landing at the top above the entrance hall. Harvey had said they'd got her in the old manager's office and the offices were at the other end of the hall overlooking the sea. Not that I'd ever been inside the place before, but Turk knew it well and had been able to give me the necessary briefing.

I could hear a guitar playing faintly some-where near at hand and the sound grew progressively louder as we moved towards the sea end of the building. No slow, haunting ballad this, but *Frankie and Johnny*, played atrociously and sung in a hoarse, broken voice.

At the far end of the gallery, we paused outside a door marked *General Office* in

Spanish. Taleb kicked on it twice and the guitar playing stopped abruptly. On my left, a narrow window looked out over the cove, its dark waters shrouded in a light mist. The moon was down.

My hands were shaking slightly, ready for action and I took a deep breath and tried to steady them. It was just like getting ready to fly another mission. No matter how good you were or how many times you'd done it before, it was always an open-ended situation where anything could happen and probably would.

The door opened and one of the Terrible Twins stood there, clutching his guitar in one hand. His mouth gaped when he saw me. Beyond him there were a couple of desks, a chair or two and a filing cabinet against the wall. There was dust everywhere, thickly coated, but the legend *Manager* in Spanish on the door behind a small wooden railing was still clear enough.

Taleb shoved him out of the way and led the way in. 'Where is your brother?'

His answer was a sudden, muffled cry from

the other room. He crossed the office in three quick strides. 'Tyler!' he called and kicked on the door.

There was silence and then a key rattled in the lock and Tyler, as Taleb had called him, peered through, the specimen who'd got the jeep door in his face the previous night.

When he saw me, something sparked in his eyes like a fuse slow-burning. 'What's he doing here?' he demanded.

He had that kind of voice described by someone once as being roughened by years of liquor and disease and the smell once again at close quarters was quite overpowering.

Taleb kicked the door in so roughly that Tyler staggered back several paces. 'What have you been up to?'

The only furniture in the room was an old army cot covered by a couple of dirty grey blankets and a single wooden chair. Sister Claire stood against the wall, her face very white. She wasn't afraid, I don't think fear was something she even understood, but there was certainly a general air of desperation to her and she was breathing hard.

Taleb said furiously, 'Didn't I tell you to leave her alone?'

'Hell, man, I was only trying to spark her some,' Tyler told him.

In the same moment Sister Claire said, 'Mr Nelson. What happened?'

She took a step towards me and Taleb produced his revolver and got in between us. 'Sit down, please.'

She looked at me searchingly, he put a hand on her shoulder and pushed her down into the chair. 'I asked you a question earlier this evening which you refused to answer. I will ask you again.'

'And my answer will still be the same,' she said.

'Which will be most unfortunate for Mr Nelson.'

She turned to me slowly. I said, 'I think he means it, angel.'

'But I can't,' she said in a low, desperate voice. 'You know that. You must know.'

'I see.' Taleb shrugged. 'Then if that is your last word, it would seem Mr Nelson must be prepared to suffer a little for the faith.'

He nodded to Tyler. 'Cut off his right ear.' He looked down at Sister Claire. 'Will that do for starters?'

'Merciful heaven, no!' she said, but Tyler had already produced a gutting knife that was twin to the one Harvey had used earlier in the evening.

He rushed me in the same split second before I was ready for him. Sister Claire cried out. I got a hand to his right wrist just in time, shoving the knife to one side and went back across the bed, the great stinking weight of him on top of me.

I was aware of his brother howling in delight from the doorway, but for a while, all was confusion, Tyler slobbering like an animal. And then I got my right hand down to the butt of Turk's Browning, so carefully taped to the inside of my left leg just above the ankle, tore it free and rammed the muzzle into Tyler's chest just below the ribcage. I pulled the trigger twice, the shots lifting him back against Taleb.

As I came to my feet Taleb, shoved him towards me, turned and ran for the open door, crowding Tyler's brother before him. I shoved the body to one side, crossed the room in a couple of strides, slammed the door shut and locked it.

When I turned, Sister Claire was on her knees beside Tyler. Whether he was still with us was debatable, but in any event, she was reciting the prayers for the dying.

'Go Christian soul in the name of God the Father Almighty who created thee . . .'

A couple of shots splintered through the door and ricocheted from the far wall. I picked up the chair and smashed it through the window, glass splinters and wood fragments showering everywhere.

Three more shots came through the door in quick succession and Tyler's brother roared incoherently and kicked at the panelling.

I pulled Sister Claire to her feet. 'No time for that. We've got to get moving. We're on what you might call a strict time schedule.'

I scrambled over the low sill, turned and handed her through. We were on a long steel landing at the front of the building, high above the grain chutes dropping down to the harbour.

I leaned over the rail and fired once into the air, something else from the old China Coast Signal Book, according to the Turk. I was answered instantly by a green flare from the darkness below.

Somewhere to the left of us a door crashed open and I grabbed her hand and started to run along the iron landing. There was a hoarse cry, two rapid shots as we reached the doorway which took us down to the iron catwalk below, stretching out from the grain chutes above the sea.

There was an instant reply from the harbour below as we started down the stairway, a single white flare which soared into the night illuminating the entire harbour. In its light, I saw the *Mary Grant* lying fifty yards out from the pier.

There was a howl of agony like some beast in pain as we reached the bottom of the stairway and started out on the catwalk and I looked up and saw Tyler's twin leaning over the rail, staring down at us in the harsh, white light.

Taleb was beside him. He fired once, obviously emptying his revolver and jumped back out of sight to reload as I replied. As for Tyler's brother, God knows what got into him, rage, I suppose, or grief, for he clambered over the rail and jumped.

He missed the catwalk and landed on the rounded head of one of the grain elevators. His feet went from under him, I had a last vivid impression of the great ugly face, mouth open in a snarl, hands clawing desperately for a grip on the smooth surface and then he simply slid back over the edge.

The light from the flare was beginning to fade as I grabbed her hand again and pulled her to the end of the catwalk. The gate on the end was secured by a chain and I pulled out the retaining pin and kicked it open.

It was perhaps forty feet down to the dark waters through the fading light and the safety of the *Mary Grant* which was already beginning to move in. And, brave to the bitter end of things, she never hesitated. As another bullet ricocheted from the rail beside us, she took my hand in hers and we jumped.

167

One of the bad things about making a parachute drop by night is the fact that you can't gauge your impact point properly. All in all, it's the quickest way of buying a broken leg I know.

It was the same now and that drop into total darkness as the last light from the flare was extinguished was anything but pleasant. It seemed to go on for rather a long time and then we hit the surface with a solid, forceful smack and kept right on going.

I lost Sister Claire's hand as we went under, but caught hold of a sleeve and kicked like hell so that when we finally broke through to the surface, we were still together.

A spotlight picked us out of the water and was instantly switched off as a shot echoed through the night from up above. The *Mary Grant* loomed out of the darkness and I grabbed for the bottom rung of the ladder Turk had thoughtfully placed in position.

Sister Claire floated beside me, her robes drifting in a circle about her. I pulled her on to the ladder and Turk leaned over the rail.

'Okay, Duchess, let's have you.'

I gave her a push from behind, just to help things along, then followed wearily, suddenly rather tired. When I hauled myself over the rail, she was crouched on deck sobbing for breath. Turk was back in the wheel-house and as I flopped down beside her, the *Mary Grant* moved away with a surge of speed.

High up above in the darkness there was another sudden spark, a bullet buried itself in the water somewhere to the right of us. But it was too late. All finished. The final bell and a moment later, we were through the passage and moving out to sea.

I was on my second large whisky when Turk came down to the saloon. He leaned in the doorway and looked me over as he lit a cigarette.

'Sounded like you had a hot time up there. What happened?'

I gave it to him in detail. When I was finished his only comment was, 'A pity you couldn't have got Taleb.'

'What about the one who peeled off the top of the grain chute?'

'Hit the edge of the dock before the water. Must have broken every bone in his body.' He shock his head. 'Man, that was one hell of a sight, I'm telling you, you and her standing on the edge up there just before the light went. How's your leg?'

It was beginning to hurt like hell, but I never liked to admit that to anyone, not even Turk.

'Fine – just fine.'

'I bet it is.'

The door to the aft cabin opened and Sister Claire came out. She wore a towel tied around her head like a turban, and an old beachrobe of Turk's.

She was very, very pale, but managed a wan smile. 'It seems I must thank you again, Mr Nelson, and you also Mr Turkovich.'

'Turk, Duchess,' he said. 'How many times have I got to tell you? It was nothing. Anybody with guts and intelligence could do the same.'

She sat down with great care to avoid

falling down or so it seemed to me and said, 'But how did you know where to find me?'

'Oh, we acted on information we received,' I replied quickly before Turk could say anything.

'I see.' She frowned. 'But I still don't understand how Mr Turkovich came to be waiting so providentially in the harbour.'

'Nothing to it, Duchess,' he said. 'What we used to call contingency planning in Vietnam.'

'We had three alternatives,' I said. 'All based on me getting up to that office, but all slightly open ended. Number one was to simply try and get you out on your own two feet and up the road to where I'd left the jeep. Number two was to make the big jump and Turk waiting.'

'And the third alternative?'

'I should have thought that was obvious.'

'To kill them, you mean? All of them.' She sighed. 'You did kill Tyler, didn't you? And his brother fell to his death.'

'Something like that.'

She got to her feet and there was a kind of anger in her voice when she said, 'Is there only violence in you, Mr Nelson? Is that your only answer?'

A remark so astonishing, considering what she had escaped by a hairsbreadth, that it left me speechless with astonishment.

Before even Turk could reply, she said, 'You must excuse me now,' and left us.

I poured myself another whisky, the neck of the bottle rattling on the glass. Turk put a hand on my shoulder. 'Don't take it to heart, General, she's as nutty as a fruit-cake. Anyway, where to now?'

'We'll use the harbour at Lillie's place,' I said. 'Make final preparations in the morning and leave around noon.'

'I hear and obey, O great one.'

He went up the companionway. I sat there for a moment longer, feeling curiously alone and then I became aware that someone was talking in a low voice. I stood up and tiptoed out past the galley.

The door to the aft cabin was slightly ajar. I could just see Sister Claire through the gap. She was on her knees. She was also praying.

7

Dark Passage

When I went up the long zig-zag of concrete steps that climbed the cliffs to the Villa Rose, I had Sister Claire's sodden habit over one arm and carried a canvas holdall. As for Sister Claire herself, she climbed ahead of me, but only with great difficulty and when we reached the back gate and I pressed the bell, I noticed that she leaned against the wall as if for support. Not that I felt so good myself and my bad leg ached like hell.

After a while there were footsteps, a nasty snuffling sound, which could only be the Alsatian. The door opened to reveal not only Jose and the dog, but Carlo who was holding an automatic shotgun in a most businesslike way.

We moved inside, the old man kicking at the dog to still it. Carlo barred the door behind us and we went up through the garden to where Lillie waited, leaning over the balustrade of the terrace.

'So you made it?' she said. 'What happened to Turk?'

'He's fine. Staying on board the *Mary Grant* tonight, just in case.'

Sister Claire made it to the terrace and reached out quickly for support and Lillie got an arm around her. For once in her life she actually managed to look concerned about another human being.

'Heh, you don't look so good,' she said. 'What happened? Did you leave anyone still moving back there?'

'Table, for one,' I said. 'But sleep is all she needs.' I passed the soaking habit to Carlo. 'If you could get the old lady to wash and iron that for the morning it would help.'

He and Lillie went out, Sister Claire between them. I left the canvas holdall on a table in the corner of the terrace, went down to the salon and raided the bar. I found a bottle of Irish whiskey called Antrim Glen which sounded promising and took it back to the terrace along with a soda syphon and a cut glass tumbler. It tasted as if it had been made in Japan, but I was at that stage when it didn't really matter. I was examining the Admiralty chart of the Khufra Marshes area when Lillie returned.

'What in hell did they do to her?'

'Nothing much. We arrived in the nick of time, trumpets blowing.'

I poured another whiskey. She said, 'That stuff I keep for people I don't want to come back again.'

'Well, you know what they say,' I told her. 'You should never go back to anything.'

I had another look at the chart and she sat on the arm of the chair beside me. 'You're crazy, Jack. Crazy, to go, I mean. Come to that, you don't even know where you're going till she decides to trust you enough.'

I traced a pencil circle around Zarza. 'It can't be too far from there, that's certain.'

'I once did a movie on location in the Florida Everglades,' she said. 'If it's anything like that, you're kidding yourselves.'

'You take a chance every day of your life,' I told her, as I folded the map. 'Anyway, we'll be off your hands around noon tomorrow. You can go back to Clock Patience and lover boy after that.'

Her hands were in my hair. She said softly, 'This is no way to say goodbye, lover. I've known you do better.'

'On any other occasion an irresistible offer, but not tonight, Josephine,' I said. 'Duty calls.'

I opened the canvas holdall, produced a Sterling submachine gun which I put down on the table, then I took out a heavy seaman's reefer jacket.

As I pulled it on she said incredulously, 'You mean you're going to stay out here all night on guard.'

'Something like that.'

'But what about me?'

'Come off it, Lillie,' I said. 'If you can't sleep or feel like a little action in the middle of the night there's always the chauffeur.'

Her reply was not at all to the point and as usual, quite unprintable. I kissed her on the cheek tenderly and went down the steps into the garden, the Sterling under my arm.

The night passed entirely without incident. As they say, I saw the dawn come in and a little after seven o'clock, squeezed a rather splendid breakfast out of old Isabel when she appeared in the kitchen.

Carlo was stirring by then and I got him to let me out of the back gate. When I was halfway down the steps to the *Mary Grant* I saw Turk appear on deck. He was drying himself off with a towel as I reached the beach.

'You look like death only very slightly warmed up,' he said as I drew close. 'What kind of night did you have?'

'Quiet – and you?'

'The same. How about the leg?'

A question which always irritated me. 'All right, so the piano needs oiling. It'll survive.'

'All right. All right.' He held up a hand.

'Suit yourself, General, only a little sleep wouldn't come amiss from the look of you.'

'I'll try that this afternoon when we're at sea,' I told him. 'But now, there's work to be done.'

'I can eat, you don't mind that?'

'Five minutes.'

'I love you, too.'

He turned and went down the companionway.

We checked out the stores again and stowed away the compressed air bottles we'd taken on board the previous night. Then there was the compressor to check and the old regulation diving suit with the brass helmet that he liked to keep around for emergencies.

By ten-thirty, we'd cleared off most of the odd jobs and were down in the engine room. There hadn't been a sign of anyone from the Villa Rose and then, when I went up on deck for an oil can, I found Sister Claire on the pier.

Her habit had been beautifully washed and

ironed, probably old Isabel's work and the white collar and hood were spotless.

'Morning,' I said. 'How do you feel?'

'Not too bad, Mr Nelson. What time do we leave?'

I turned to Turk who'd come up to join me. 'What do you think?'

'We can make it for noon if you like.'

'Good.' She smiled palely. 'I have time to go to church then.'

'Like hell you do,' I said forcefully.

'But Mr Nelson, there is a church at San Jose. I wouldn't need to go into Ibiza town.'

'Nothing doing.'

She seemed paler than ever, the eyes very dark in the white face. 'Please, Mr Nelson, it is most necessary for me to make my Confession before I leave. You understand? In case anything should happen . . .'

'To hell with your Confession,' I said.

She was obviously badly shocked and stood there, staring at me, 'Oh, my dear friend,' she said. 'How can I have offended you so?'

I couldn't think of any kind of reply to

that. In any case, there was no need for Turk picked up his shirt and stepped over the rail to join her.

'No sweat, Duchess, I'll take you.'

He took her by the elbow, she turned strangely reluctant and they moved away together. There are some mornings when you can't win. That was one of them very definitely. I went back down into the engine room.

About eleven-thirty, I was washing off on deck when I was hailed from the steps and looked up to see Lillie half-way down. She wore a broad brimmed straw hat, the sort of thing local women used when working in the fields, a bikini top and scarlet beach pants. She was also carrying a basket.

'Any sign of Turk and Sister Claire?' I asked her as she stepped over the rail.

'Not since they left for San Jose. He borrowed the station wagon. Told me you were definitely leaving at noon.' She opened the basket which proved to contain a couple of bottles of French champagne bedded in ice. 'I thought we might say goodbye in the proper fashion. Did I tell you M.G.M. want me for the lead in a great new movie?'

I popped the cork and filled the glasses she held out. It tasted out of this world and suddenly, life was good again, a place of warmth and smells and pleasant tastes and lovely women.

'That's marvellous.' I kissed her on the mouth. 'Fell in love with you the first time I saw you through the darkness from the front row stalls, up there on that enormous silver screen.'

I poured some more champagne in her glass. She said slowly, managing to look more serious than at any time since I'd known her, 'You won't come back, Jack. You know that, don't you?'

'What is it the toreros say before going in the bull-ring?' I said. 'It comes as God wills.'

'Please, Jack, listen to me.' But she got no further for at that moment, Turk and Sister Claire appeared on the steps, Carlo behind them.

Lillie swore softly but there was nothing to

be done. As they came along the pier Turk called, 'A party? Why didn't someone tell me?'

He helped Sister Claire over the rail and Lillie said, 'Just a farewell drink, darling.'

'That's for me.'

I filled a glass for Turk but Sister Claire refused. She looked as calm as usual, but seemed very subdued.

'Can't we tempt you, darling?' Lillie asked her.

'I don't think so.' Sister Claire glanced at her watch and turned to me. 'Didn't you say noon, Mr Nelson?'

God, but there were times when I think she was the most infuriating woman I'd ever known. In the silence which followed I looked at Turk and Lillie, grinned wryly and raised my glass.

'Bottoms up.'

I tossed it over the side, Lillie and Turk followed suit. She kissed him goodbye full on the mouth, long and hard and he smacked her backside.

'May your God go with you, angel,' he said. 'You're the best there is.'

She turned to me and moved close. 'I can't make you change your mind?'

'Not a chance.'

She nodded, then kissed me gently on the cheek with great sadness, whether simulated or not I could not be sure although it had all the overtones of a bad movie.

Carlo helped her over the rail, I cast off at once and Turk started the engines. As we moved away, Lillie and Carlo turned and started towards the steps. I coiled the lines neatly as we passed out through the narrow entrance, waves slapping against the hull as Turk increased speed. It was a really beautiful day. Azure seas, cloudless blue sky, everything you could wish for.

But I was tired – damn tired. I turned from the rail and found her watching patiently. 'I think we should talk now, Mr Nelson,' she said.

There was an edge to her voice I didn't like that reminded me unpleasantly of those times you got a new C.O. who wanted to be hail-fellow-well-met, but who also wanted there to be no mistake about who was in charge.

'Not now,' I said and I brushed past her. 'Now I sleep. For at least eight hours. You hear that, Turk?'

'I hear you, General,' he called.

'But Mr Nelson . . .'

I turned and went down the companionway.

Strange how dreams insist on taking us back into the past again at a distance of years and for no good reason.

I was in the jungle again, back in Vietnam, running through the bush head-down, filled with a feeling of the most incredible panic. Whoever they were, they were closing in on me fast, invisible hounds snapping at my heels and I'd lost Turk, couldn't find him anywhere and only the Turk could save me now.

The undergrowth grew thicker, turned into an impenetrable thicket that hooked into me when I tried to break through so that I was held fast.

The hands of the damned were pulling me down, I opened my mouth in a soundless scream and sat up with a start, bathed in sweat, to find Sister Claire shaking me.

I stared at her blankly. 'What time is it?'

'A little after eight,' she said. 'I think you should relieve Mr Turkovich for a while.'

There was something in her voice. I sat up and swung my legs to the floor. 'Trouble?'

'He's trying to dry out,' she said. 'You know what that means.'

There was little of what one might term charity in her voice, certainly no compassion, but, looking back on it all now I can see what was happening to her, how her very thinking was affected. This affair was of supreme importance – so much so that nothing must be allowed to stand in its way. Certainly no person. She was willing to drive herself to the ultimate edge. It was the least she would expect from others.

'In other words what you're really trying to say is that this is no time for weakness,' I observed.

'You put it a little harshly perhaps.'

'But you'd still prefer him to have a fix.'

She didn't attempt to dodge the issue, I'll say that for her, simply looked me straight in the eye and said, 'If the circumstances warrant. Could you handle him in the Khufra, Mr Nelson, if he broke down?'

I went up the companionway and out on deck it was a fine night, still warm with only the lightest of seas running. Turk was in the wheelhouse and in the compass light, his face looked awful, older than time itself, ravaged beyond belief.

He said, 'Hi, there, General, how's every little thing?'

I said, 'You don't look so good. Anything I can get you?'

'Not me, General, never felt better.' His teeth were chattering so much he had difficulty in speaking. 'A couple of hours sleep is all I need.'

He gave me the course and moved to one side for me to take the wheel, his face shiny with sweat. I said urgently, 'This is no time to get religion for Christ's sake. You need a fix. Take one.'

'Not me, General.' He smiled like a dying man trying to say goodbye. 'Never again.'

He moved outside, walked along the deck lurching so badly that, for a moment there I thought he might go over, and went below.

Sister Claire appeared half-an-hour later with hot tea and fried egg sandwiches on a tray. She put it down on the chart table, a rather incongruous figure in such surroundings.

'How is he?' I said.

'I don't know. He went into his cabin and locked the door.'

'Maybe you'll get your wish,' I said. 'The state he was in when he left here, he didn't look as if he could last for very long.'

She said calmly, 'I meant what I said however harsh it may have sounded to you. In other circumstances I would gladly devote every waking moment to help him break free of this curse, but this is neither the time nor place.'

'Never mind, Sister,' I said. 'You make fine egg sandwiches.'

Which she did and I gave them all my attention during the rather obvious silence which followed. When I was ready, she poured me a cup of tea which proved to be easily the equal of the sandwiches.

'Excellent,' I told her.

She said, 'You don't like me very much, do you, Mr Nelson?'

'Not really,' I said cheerfully. 'But then, as you once pointed out, I don't like anybody very much.'

My leg which had been aching for quite some time, now started to hurt like hell, so much so, in fact, that I gave a sudden gasp of pain and struck at the thigh with my clenched fist.

'There is something wrong?' she said. 'You're in pain. Did you hurt yourself last night?'

I shook my head. 'No, this goes way back to dear old Vietnam. They threw me out on my ear, or didn't I tell you? Medically unfit for further flying duties.'

'I'm sorry,' she said.

And then that damned Scots Presbyterian

conscience broke through to the surface again. 'No they didn't,' I said. 'The truth is they offered me a desk job and I turned it down.'

'I see,' she said. 'It had to be flying or nothing?'

'Something like that. Maybe Turk should have left me back there in the bush.'

'I don't understand,' she said.

So I told her the story – as good a time-filler as any. When I was finished she said, 'Men are such strange creatures. The mad, gallant things they will do for each other. I see now why you are such good friends. What did you do when you left the service? Haven't you ever been married?'

And here it was, the past rearing its ugly head again, every festering sore I'd ever thought healed over ready to erupt. And yet . . .

I said, 'Oh, yes, I was married. To a girl with ash blonde hair called Sigrid who I met in Germany when I was stationed over there with the R.A.F.'

'What happened?'

'When I was posted to Vietnam she was

living in Sydney. I arranged for everything to be put in her name to make it simpler for her if anything happened to me. The house, bank account – that sort of thing. I happened to think rather a lot of her, you see.'

'Go on.'

My mouth had gone dry, so I tried some more tea. 'It's really very simple. She didn't come to see me in hospital. Finally wrote to say she'd met someone else, a German engineer who'd been over on a contract, and was going back to Hamburg with him.'

She put a hand on my arm and said softly, 'I'm very sorry, my friend.'

'But you haven't heard the best bit,' I told her. 'She cleaned me out. Sold the house, the car, cleared the bank account – screwed me into the ground and it was all legal. Now you must admit that's really rather funny.'

I don't know what she would have said to that, have no idea what was on her mind because just as she opened her mouth to speak, Turk screamed down there in his cabin.

*   *   *

I put the boat on automatic pilot, shoved Sister Claire out of the way and went down the companionway on the run.

His cabin door was locked so I kicked it hard and yelled, 'Open this bloody door, Turk.'

He screamed again and started to shout out in a kind of frenzy. 'Dear God, no! Keep away from me! Don't look at me like that! I didn't know! I didn't know!'

Sister Claire had arrived by then. She said quickly, 'He's going into delirium, Mr Nelson. He needs his usual shot as quickly as possible or he'll be in real trouble.'

I didn't need her to tell me that. I leaned back, raised my good leg and stamped against the door hard splintering the wood around the lock so that it gave suddenly, the door flying open.

Turk lay on the bunk, eyes staring madly, plucking at himself. The tin box in which he kept his drugs and hypodermic was on the side table as if he'd put them there deliberately as a kind of test.

As he started to go into convulsions I sat

on the edge of the bunk and held his arms while Sister Claire got an injection ready expertly. He grinned up at me, teeth bared, not seeing me, seeing some indefinable horror beyond and the words when they came, were broken and disjointed.

'I killed them, me, the great Turk. Killed all the little children. Harry Turkovich – butcher to the trade.'

He started to shake wildly and I leaned on him hard while she bared his arm and gave him the injection. For a moment, he seemed to go into a kind of rictus and then, suddenly, it was as if a string had been cut and he went very still.

She pulled back his lids and examined the eyes. 'He'll sleep now,' she said. 'Afterwards he'll be much better.' She covered him with a blanket and turned to me. 'What did he mean about the children, Mr Nelson?'

'God knows,' I said. 'The first time I've heard him say such a thing.'

She smoothed the hair away from his face. 'Poor man. If ever I've heard a soul in torment, it was just now.'

What was it Bertha had said? *He's a murderer, isn't he?* Suddenly it was as if I could no longer breathe and I turned, plunged out into the corridor and went up on deck.

My hands were shaking so badly that I needed to grip the wheel tightly to hold them steady. I felt like someone on the edge of darkness knowing that something terrible lurks in the shadows below and yet consumed with a fearful curiosity to discover what it is.

I needed a drink and Turk being what he was, I soon found one in the locker under the chart table. Brandy, but good stuff for a change. I didn't take too much because there was work to be done. Just enough to make me feel better. As I put down the bottle Sister Claire appeared.

'Is that really necessary, Mr Nelson?' she said. 'I would have thought we needed one clear head at least.'

'And that, Sister, depends entirely on your point of view,' I told her. 'How is he?'

'He's lousy.' Turk moved out of the

shadows behind her, a strange, biblical-looking figure with that long hair, a blanket draped around his shoulders like a cloak.

'So, the dead can walk after all?' I said.

'Something like that. Give me a cigarette, General. Tailor made if you don't mind. Nothing exotic.'

I lit one for him and passed it across. He slumped down to the deck just outside the open door of the wheelhouse, his back against the rail, his face drifting out of the darkness from time-to-time in the glow of the cigarette as he drew on it.

'I said some funny things down there. You must be wondering.'

'You weren't yourself,' Sister Claire began, but I cut in on her roughly.

'If there's anything you want to get off your chest Turk, I'd say now is as good a time as any.'

'You mean it could even be my last chance?'

He laughed, but it was not a pleasant sound. I said, 'Whatever it is, it's been tearing your insides apart for long enough.'

There was a long silence. Beyond the rail,

the sea seemed to glow with a kind of phosphorescence. Spray drifted across the windows of the wheelhouse, invisible fingers tapped nervously on the glass as if someone out there in the darkness was trying to get in.

Turk said in a calm, slow voice. 'It's soon told. It was just after the Haiphong job. Remember, General, when I was such a big hero?'

He seemed to want some kind of response so I said, 'You were, in my book.'

'There was an ammunition ship running the blockade from North Korea. The Navy lost her, then Intelligence got word she was sheltering in a bay on one of those off-shore islands near the mouth of the Red River, waiting her chance to make a run for Haiphong. And she had to be stopped, man. I mean, that one boat could have had an incalculable effect on the conduct of the entire war – just like it says in the movies.'

He was punishing himself and too much considering what he'd just been through. I said, 'Okay, Turk, get to it.'

'I am, General, I am. The best is yet to

come, believe me. I mean, this was a job for one man – a volunteer. Real *Boys Own* stuff. They dropped me by parachute with all the right gear. I swam out to the boat and slapped a couple of limpet mines to her keel. And when she blew, she blew, I'm telling you. Went down like a stone.'

'Sounds like a good job well done to me.'

'That's what I thought, so next morning, at first light, just before I was due to be picked up I swam out into the bay and dived to see how things were.'

He paused for no more than a heartbeat and went on, 'The sun was just coming up so there was plenty of light, but something was wrong, badly wrong, I knew that from the first moment. It was as if I wasn't alone. Hell, for a while, I had that feeling you get just by instinct sometimes that tells you other divers are about.' He hesitated as if considering what his next statement should be. 'Anyway, when I went below, I noticed the door to the main saloon was barred which naturally aroused my curiousity so I opened it.'

I held my breath for a moment involuntarily knowing that whatever it was, it was coming now. He said, 'When I swam into the saloon, a young girl tried to get me by the throat.'

Sister Claire, who had been utterly silent throughout the whole proceedings, gave a sudden shocked gasp. I didn't blame her. As for me, I was back at the top of the stairs, nerves tingling, waiting to see what waited down there in the darkness.

'They were everywhere,' Turk said. 'Children, dozens of them. Drifting around, arms reaching out beseeching me, hating me, terrified. God, for a moment there they were all around me, I thought I'd never get out, but I did, though how I made it back to the shore I'll never know.'

'But I don't understand,' Sister Claire said.

'Somebody made a mistake. Wrong boat. Not ammunition, just refugees. I managed to drown a couple of hundred kids in all.' He shook his head. 'And when I flew in to base the following day, I heard I'd been cited for the Congressional for the Haiphong affair.' He turned to me. 'Ain't life a ball, General? You got another cigarette?'

I gave him one and said calmly, 'Did you check the holds, Turk?'

'Now why would I do that?'

'To see if she was carrying the hard stuff.'

'You mean that makes a difference?' He laughed shortly. 'Not in my book. Not ever.'

He stood up wearily and flicked his cigarette over the rail and when he drew the blanket around his shoulders, there was a strange kind of dignity to him. 'You know what the President said when he pinned the Congressional on me, Sister? He said he'd rather be me than him.'

He started to walk away along the deck and paused, 'Don't you think that's the funniest thing you ever did hear?'

As he went below, Sister Claire started to cry quietly.

8

Coast of Danger

The weather started to break soon after that and I had other things on my mind. Not that it was anything to worry about. Winds three to four with rain squalls according to the radio, but the sky did become overcast very quickly and the waves, breaking into white-caps, made for a much more uncomfortable ride.

We were closing in on the Algerian coast now, not much more than an hour by estimation. I was checking the chart again closely when the door flew open and Sister Claire staggered in clutching a coffee pot and a couple of tin cups.

She got the door closed quickly and leaned

against it, looking even more incongruous than she had previously wearing a sou'wester with a yellow oilskin over her habit against the rain.

'Rough weather,' she said and moved to the chart table where, not without difficulty, she poured coffee into one of the cups.

'I've seen worse. Where's Turk?'

'In his cabin again.' She hesitated. 'I don't know what to do. What to say to him.'

'Nothing,' I said. 'If you have any sense. Could be he's already regretting having opened his mouth.'

'I would have thought it might have helped him.'

'Confession being good for the soul?' I shook my head. 'Not for him, Sister.'

'But that's not good enough,' she said. 'He was as much a victim as those children – in every way. Surely you must see that.'

'In my book, yes, but not in his. Turk sees himself as only one thing – mass murderer. The Medal of Honor only made it worse. He'll feel like that till the day he dies.'

'So tried to kill himself a little bit more

each day, is that what you mean? Progressive suicide?'

'Not at all,' I said. 'Expiation is a word that fits the circumstances much more readily. I'd have thought that something you would have understood.'

At that moment the door crashed open again and Turk appeared. He closed it quickly and said cheerfully, 'We're in luck. The right kind of weather for the approach. Do I smell coffee?'

He was completely his old self which didn't surprise me because when he brushed past to stand at the chart table, I could smell brandy.

He swallowed some of the coffee she gave him and spread the Khufra Marshes chart out on the table. 'All right, let's review the situation. Taleb is still in Ibiza and with any luck, that's where he thinks we are.'

'Which means we could be in and out before he knows it?' I said.

'Exactly, only I don't think it would pay to take a chance on that. Wouldn't you think it likely he'd be in touch with his people in

Algiers to keep a watch at the mouth of the Khufra River anyway?'

'Which is the only navigable way into the marshes.'

He tapped at the chart with a pencil. 'On paper – yes. Remember I told you I ran cigarettes for an outfit near here a time or two?'

'That's right. So what?'

'On a couple of occasions we rendezvoused in a lagoon about a mile inside the marshes. They gave me a pilot, some local fisherman, who showed me the channel.'

'A back way in?'

'Something like that. It'll be a pretty hairy experience. Those sandbanks change all the time, but I think we can make it. Once inside they'll never find us among those reeds, even from the air, especially if we use the camouflage net I've got in the hold. After all, there's ten thousand square miles of marsh to go at. Real needle in the haystack stuff.' He threw down the pencil. 'One thing's for sure. If anyone's hanging about at the mouth of the Khufra, they'll have a long wait.'

'Looks good to me,' I turned to Sister Claire. 'All right, Sister, this is where you make your contribution. The big moment.'

She rattled off a cross bearing without the slightest hesitation. Turk worked quickly, marking it on the chart. When he was finished, he turned to me. 'Better check it. Two and two make five on some days of the week as far as I'm concerned.'

I went to work with the parallel rulers and dividers and came up with exactly the same result. I drew a pencil ring around the position. 'Three miles north-east of Zarza.'

He turned to Sister Claire. 'The people I used to deal with told me there were some pretty wild characters living in the Khufra. Husa, was that the name of the tribe?'

She nodded. 'A strange people. Something of a throw-back. Wild, Berber horsemen, just like the old days. The authorities can do little with them.'

'Horsemen?' I said. 'In marsh country?'

'Oh, yes, it has been so for generations. The horses have been specially bred to it. They swim as well as they gallop.'

'Do any of these characters hang out in Zarza?' Turk asked her.

She shook her head. 'Zarza is only a poor place. A village on an island in a lagoon. Proof fishermen mostly. Wild fowlers. That sort of thing.'

'Do the Husa ever give them any trouble?'

'Occasionally, but not often. The people of Zarza and places like it know the marshes too well. They can melt into the background whenever it suits them. And they are good, gentle people. No one could have been kinder than they were to Talif and me.'

'Which is all very cosy,' I said. 'But we still want to keep out of their way if it's at all possible. We go in, get what we came for and come out again just as fast as we can.' I looked at Turk. 'What do you think? Two days?'

'I don't see why not. There can't be more than five fathoms of water in any of these inland lagoons so there's no need to worry about decompression times and so on, but both of us will have to dive.'

'Fair enough,' I said.

He turned to Sister Claire. 'Which brings us to you, Duchess. Plenty of hard work for you up top, operating the diesel winch to bring the stuff up. I'll show you. It's simple enough.'

'I came prepared to do my share, Mr Turkovich,' she said.

'But not in that outfit, I hope.'

'I came prepared for that also.'

'Good, then as you're the only one of us who hasn't had any rest, I suggest you go below while there's still time. I'll let you know when it's zero hour.'

She was obviously reluctant and hesitated so Turk opened the door and gave her a slight push. 'Why don't you try doing as you're told for a change?'

She actually laughed at that, but she went. When he closed the door and turned to me, I said, 'What was that all about?'

'I wanted her out of the way, that's all.'

'Why?'

'Let's just say this back way into the Khufra that I mentioned is going to be anything but a joyride. In fact if we're to stand any kind of a chance, we're going to have to know that chart backwards so let's get started.'

Within an hour, we were moving in to the coast. It was raining intermittently now, but there was a certain amount of fog about, drifting out to sea, pushed by a stiff offshore breeze.

Turk leaned over the chart. '*Strong currents constantly changing. Not to be relied on*,' he said. 'I know what that means. One day there's a sandbank or maybe just six fathoms of clear water. You can never be sure. These marsh estuary areas are the same all over the world.'

For the moment the *Mary Grant* was on automatic pilot and I leaned over the chart beside him. What made this whole section of the coast particularly hazardous was a great reef called the Hogsback which was so long it actually ran off the chart we were using.

'I can't see any route through that lot.'

'Like I told you, General, not on paper,

but there is one.' He tapped with a pencil. 'See this island – Boukhari? All it is is a damn great rock sticking up out of the reef like a sore finger. Two or maybe three hundred feet high. There's a passage on the east side.'

'Which isn't marked.'

'Two fathoms of water,' he said. 'It's enough. I've been through twice. It can be done. Coming out's easy, by the way.'

'I'm happy to hear that, but I think you'd better explain the trick of getting in.'

It was simple enough. There was an automatic light beyond the reef at the far end of the marsh. Ten miles beyond it there was a lighthouse near Cape Djinet. By coincidence, a course inland keeping those two lights directly in line took you straight through Turk's channel.

In other words, all you needed was perfect visibility, good weather, seamanship amounting to genius and lots and lots of luck.

By one a.m. we were close inshore, running without lights. The sky was clear again, on fire with stars and the moon, riding high in the mid-heaven, made visibility excellent.

We were running parallel with the reef and I saw now how it had earned its name of Hogsback for it ran westward into the night in an unbroken chain of jagged rocks and white water. I could feel the turbulence as we moved in closer, waves slapping solidly against the *Mary Grant*'s hull.

Turk held the wheel lightly, his face, from what I could see of it in the compass light, calm and relaxed and yet he seemed ready for anything, capable of anything. I suppose I knew, quite suddenly in that moment, that we were going to get through. That there was no doubt of it. That I was watching a master at work.

'There she blows,' he said suddenly.

I went out on deck and stood at the rail and saw perhaps a couple of hundred yards away, a great, jagged, black pinnacle rearing into the night.

And then we were so close that I could see white water boiling in a frenzy across the great rocks at its base. I turned to go back in the wheelhouse, lost my balance and fell back against the rail as Turk shouted a warning.

He swung the wheel hard to port, giving the engines full power at the same moment. As I hung on to the rail for dear life, I saw that we were entering a narrow band of clear water, Boukhari towering on one side, the jagged white and black carpet of the reef on the other.

All around us, broken rocks were appearing and disappearing in a welter of foam. The turbulence of the water was fantastic, like great hammer blows on the hull and at one point, for one terrifying moment we slewed to starboard.

I could see Turk through the open door of the wheelhouse fighting for control. We slowed very obviously, presumably a sandbank although it felt like running into a solid wall and then quite suddenly, we were free and moving through clear water.

Turk leaned out of the door. 'What did I tell you, General, nothing to it.'

'That will do me for tonight,' I said. 'Or have you anything else up your sleeve?'

'Nothing too difficult. We've got to get undercover, that's the main thing. There's a lagoon about half a mile in. If we can make it to there we should be safe enough. We can carry on at first light.'

He reduced speed to five or six knots and we moved on into the night.

I was aware of the harsh, pungent smell of the marsh now and wild fowl and sea birds bedded down for the night, stirred protestingly as we moved in through the sandbanks.

The route seemed plain enough and we followed it for half a mile or so and then most of the sandbanks disappeared and we were faced by a vast expanse of dark water, the edge of the marsh on the other side.

'This is where it usually gets tricky,' Turk said. 'You can never tell what's underneath here. It changes every other day.'

But on the whole, we hadn't much trouble. Twice we grounded but he was able to get us off with his engines. Only once did we really get stuck and I had to strip and go over the side, chest-deep, to help her on.

God, but it was cold and by the time we'd got her off and I pulled myself up the ladder and over the rail, my leg was hurting again.

'Good work, General,' Turk called softly.

I went below, towelled myself dry and got the whisky out. There wasn't a sound from Sister Claire so I went back on deck quietly.

Everything had changed. We were moving along a narrow channel, barely wide enough to take the boat, great dark walls rustling in the night on either side.

I reached out to trail my fingers along the reeds and Turk called, 'Quite something, aren't they?'

A moment later, we entered a small lagoon, he cut the engines and let the *Mary Grant* drift into the reed bed at the far end. 'Okay, General, this is it. I'll get the net.'

He was back in a few moments and we untied the camouflage net and unrolled it between us. God knows where he'd got it from for it had obviously been Army issue at some time or other, but it was certainly just right for the job and by the time we'd finished we had enclosed the entire boat.

'That's it, then,' he said. 'Four or five hours sleep and we move on at first light.'

'Sounds good to me. It's been quite a night.'

The door to the companionway opened and Sister Claire appeared. 'Where are we?' she demanded. 'What's happening?'

'You tell her,' Turk said. 'I'm bushed,' and he went below.

The night teemed with life around us. Odd birds still protesting, the sound of the cicadas and a bullfrog croaked noisily near at hand.

She gave a very obvious start. 'What on earth was that?'

'A bullfrog, Sister,' I told her. 'Commonly found in salt marshes the world over. I suppose, in a way, you could say you've come home.'

And at that, I gave her good night and followed Turk below.

9

The Pot of Gold

I was awake at six to find grey light filtering in through the portholes. Turk was still asleep, head pillowed on one arm and his face, in repose, seemed even more gaunt and fleshless than usual. I wondered just how long he had left, but that was entirely the wrong way to start the day and I forced the thought away.

There wasn't a sound from Sister Claire's cabin so I padded out through the saloon, made some coffee and went up on deck with a cup in one hand and the coffee pot in the other.

It was a grey, sombre morning, the sky very overcast, rain in the offing from the appearance of things. I clambered up on top of the wheelhouse and peered through the camouflage net.

It was a scene as wild and desolate as I have ever known, mile upon mile of these great reeds stretching into the distance, the only sound, the strange, eerie whispering of the wind as it moved among them.

I dropped back down to the deck, reached for my coffee and Sister Claire said, 'Did you see anything?'

She was wearing jeans and an old sweater and her cropped hair was covered by an old stocking cap of the type worn by commandos. She looked strangely vulnerable, out of uniform, so to speak, and very young.

I said, 'We're the last people left on top of earth.'

'I know.' She nodded. 'It affects one that way, this place. Lonely from the beginning of time until now.'

'That sounds like poetry.' I poured more coffee into the cup and passed it to her.

She held it in both hands while she drank. Overhead a skein of wild geese drifted across the grey sky in a V formation.

She said, 'They're beautiful, aren't they? So free.'

I could not help but put the obvious question, 'And you're not?'

She side-stepped me neatly. 'We all have responsibilities, Mr Nelson. What I am, I choose to be. We all have a choice. We are what we are because we allow it to happen.'

Which seemed a pretty harsh way of looking at things. 'That doesn't seem to leave much room for what your people term charity.'

'All the room in the world, my friend, but sentimentality helps no one. Change – real changes – come from within the self. Not from outside. And everything does change. Nothing stays the same.'

'Sounds more like Buddhism than Christianity to me,' I commented.

'Then I can only suggest that you go back to a more detailed reading of the Scriptures, Mr Nelson.'

Turk appeared from the companionway at that moment, putting an end to the conversation. He wore a heavy sweater against the cold air, but otherwise was bright and cheerful enough, which could only mean he'd had a fix and the bright patch of unnatural colour in each cheek confirmed it.

'I smell coffee.'

Sister Claire gave him her cup and I filled it for him. 'As you see I am ready for work,' she said.

He looked her over gravely then nodded. 'Yes, I like it. I don't know what the Vatican will say, but it's definitely you.'

He climbed up on top of the wheelhouse and peered out over the desolate landscape. He had a compass on a cord around his neck which he checked quickly then looked out over the marshes again.

When he jumped down to the deck he seemed remarkably cheerful. 'Eight miles, General, that's what I make it. South by south-west.'

'What about breakfast?' Sister Claire said.

'To hell with breakfast,' he said. 'The sooner we start, the sooner we're there.'

He swallowed the rest of his coffee, went into the wheelhouse and a moment later the engines rumbled protestingly into life.

*   *   *

216

It was a strange journey and curiously time-less in a way, things happening in slow motion as we moved through a maze of narrow waterways, threading our way delicately through the reeds.

And when the sun started to climb, it carried with it a furnace heat that brought the marsh alive in a way it hadn't been before. There were birds everywhere, wild duck, widgeon, geese, and mosquitoes hovered in great clouds. And the smell of the place at times was un-believable, as if the whole world rotted.

Turk stayed at the wheel and I took up a position on top of the wheelhouse with a pair of fieldglasses, searching the country ahead for a route through.

It was constantly necessary to go back the way we had come and try another way, some-times going off in what seemed like entirely the wrong direction.

On several occasions, we stuck fast and I had to go over the side into that stinking black gumbo to help things along while Turk reversed the engine. When that didn't work he had to give the wheel to Sister Claire and join me.

217

In short, two hours of hell was enjoyed by all before we finally slowed to a halt in a narrow creek between the reeds and Turk cut the engine. I was standing in the prow at the time with Sister Claire and as the *Mary Grant* drifted to a halt against a wall of reeds, Turk emerged from the wheel-house.

'This is it, folks.'

Sister Claire shook her head, 'No, it can't be. It was a much larger expanse of water than this. A lagoon.'

It came to me suddenly and with a sense of shock, that she could have been wrong from the beginning. She had been so sure of her facts. So certain of the cross-bearing Jaeger had given her as he died. Yet what had we had to go on, after all, but the memory of a young girl afraid in the dark?

Turk said cheerfully, 'No sweat, Duchess, you crashed at night – right?' She nodded and he went on, 'What happened then?'

'I was in the water, deep water. I don't really remember getting out of the plane and then Talif appeared beside me with one of those inflatable rubber dinghies. He got me into it and we paddled across the lagoon into the reeds.'

'You didn't hang around?'

'We didn't realise until later what a desolate place it was. Talif was afraid that someone might have seen the crash and come looking. To get as far away as possible from the scene seemed the most sensible thing to do.'

Turk looked at me and shrugged. 'Okay, General, we'd better take a look.'

We climbed on top of the wheelhouse and stood back-to-back, taking a section each. The situation immediately looked more promising for there was open water in two or three places on either side.

We dropped back to the deck and Turk unbuttoned his shirt. 'I'll go left, you go right and we'll see what we can find.'

'Is there anything I can do?' Sister Claire asked.

'There certainly is. You can give us a call every couple of minutes, just so we know where home is.'

Going over the side at that point was nothing like as unpleasant as it had been earlier. The water was certainly earthy enough, but pleasantly cool after the heat. I selected a narrow waterway that snaked through the reeds and followed it for quite a while, finally coming out into a patch of water no more than five or six yards across.

The only item of interest it contained was a large, vermilion water snake which slipped past me at considerable speed, giving me my worst moment since running the passage through the reef the previous night. There was nothing to do but to retrace my course and try again.

I followed three or four more channels through the reeds with no visible result except to disturb the wild life of the place considerably.

Sister Claire's voice pulled me back unfailingly to my starting point each time, but to say that I was beginning to get worried was something of an understatement. I kept thinking of a dying man in the dusk, senses failing, and wondered just how accurate he could possibly be.

And then Turk's voice sounded high and clear from the other side of the waterway.

To follow the sound of it, I had to swim directly into a wall of reeds, forcing my way through for certainly at that point there was no clear route to follow. I broke through and found myself on the edge of a lagoon that was roughly circular in shape and must have been two or three hundred feet in diameter.

It was a quiet place. No birds sang there, no frogs croaked. Just still, dark water among the heavy reeds, clear as glass all the way down to a sandy bottom.

I suppose I knew then that Jaeger had been as close as any man could be under the circumstances. That we had reached our destination.

As I swam forward Turk surfaced forty or fifty feet away, the long, wet hair clinging to his face like seaweed.

'Over here, General,' he called softly.

I joined him and saw the Heron at once down there on the floor of the lagoon.

By nine-thirty we had the *Mary Grant* firmly anchored in the right position. Sister Claire looked pale and had to some extent withdrawn into herself from the moment we had entered the lagoon, forcing a way through the reed barrier with the engines on half power. But it was understandable enough. This place had painful memories and there was something else to be considered. Something we had all avoided mentioning. The fact that not only gold and silver was waiting down there, but whatever remained of her father and Jaeger. But Turk was a different man. The brisk professional coming to terms with what he knew best.

'It couldn't be better,' he said. 'Five to six fathoms is all. We'll take a look together.'

We didn't bother with wet suits, not for that first dive for the heat by now was so intense that to drop over the rail into the cool water was a distinct pleasure. I paused to adjust my air supply and went down in a long sweeping curve after him.

The Heron had rolled over on to her side, her starboard wing tilted towards the surface for she had lost the port wing entirely, presumably on impact and it lay some little distance away, both engines still intact.

The main body of the aircraft showed every sign of the trouble she had run into on that dark night so long ago, fuselage punctured by giant tears, presumably cannon and shredded by heavy machine gun fire. It seemed a miracle that anyone had got out at all.

Turk was up by the nose. He beckoned to me and when I joined him I found more impact damage to the cabin roof and windows crushed together in a tangled mass. It was impossible to get inside but when I peered in, I saw a skull in what was left of an old fashioned leather flying helmet and the shoulder holster was still strapped into place.

Piet Jaeger. A great black-bearded man, who seemed to laugh all the time and wore a shoulder holster. Wasn't that what she'd said? *The most romantic figure I'd ever seen in my life.*

Dust to dust. I turned to look for Turk, found that he had already left me and was down on the floor of the lagoon on the port side. He beckoned again then turned his thumb down. I knew why the moment I joined him for one result of the aircraft's sharp tilt to port had been to make any kind of entrance by way of the main door impossible.

We sat on deck in the hot sun and drank the coffee Sister Claire provided. Turk wasn't in the least despondent.

'No sweat,' he said. 'We've got two choices. We can blast a way in or we can burn.'

'Blasting would be quicker,' I said.

'And noisier. Another thing, underwater explosions are funny things. You can never be absolutely certain what's going to happen.'

'In other words, we could end up worse off than we are now?'

'That's about the size of it.'

'All right, so we cut our way in. Do you want me to handle it?'

'It's an idea. It would leave me free to come and go in case of snags. I think you should wear the regulation suit though.' He turned to Sister Claire. 'You can act as diver's tender, Duchess. The most important job on board.'

'What do I have to do?'

'Handle his lifeline and airhose. Make sure the compressor keeps banging away.'

'I'll do my best,' she said.

He laughed grimly. 'You'd better, Sister, or you'll have a dead man on your hands. Now let's get to it.'

Divers and aircraft pilots have two things in common. They're both engaged in occupations which are totally alien to the species which probably explains the enormous attraction of both of them.

The difference between Turk and myself was that he loved his work. I could take it or leave it. I'd helped him when the situation demanded on previous occasions, mostly

225

shallow water work with an aqualung, but I had gone down in the old canvas and rubber regulation suit with the lead boots and brass helmet once before.

A memorable if rather unpleasant experience. I could still taste the stale air when I had a mind to, tainted with the sour smell of fresh urine, for divers frequently find they are unable to hold their bladders at depth.

Turk, as I've said, loved everything to do with his art, had every item of equipment necessary to the operation laid out on the deck while Sister Claire helped me into the suit. He started the compressor, checked the lines, then lifted the great brass helmet carefully over my head and locked it firmly.

'You okay, General?'

'What do you think?' I said sourly.

He grinned. 'That's the spirit. I'll join you down there when I'm sure the Duchess can handle things all right.'

He screwed the face plate into place, cutting off any further conversation. I got to my feet and clumped to the gap in the rail and stood at the head of the ladder. Then he thumped me in the back and I stepped in. I went down in slow motion, landing in a cloud of sand. I paused to get my bearings and check my valves and then the cutter dropped down beside me on the end of its tube.

An oxy-hydrogen cutter is ignited from the surface, gases passing down the tube to where an ingenious device allows air to bleed out forming an air bubble, an artificial atmosphere inside which the flame burns.

I lumbered across to the plane in slow motion going round to the starboard side, which seemed the obvious thing to do, and waited. A moment later Turk appeared beside me. He grinned through his mask, went up top again. After a while, the cutter ignited and I went to work.

It wasn't too difficult. The flame cut into the fuselage easily enough and Turk appeared to hover at my side again to see how things were going. He left me for a while, prowling around the body of the plane, pausing once high above my head to examine the sharply tilted starboard wing, holding on to the tip.

I could have sworn there was a tremor

through the water and the Heron seemed to move slightly. An optical illusion surely for Turk, apparently satisfied, was on his way back to the surface.

I returned to my work, by now perhaps halfway round the circuit. I paused after another five minutes, picked up the crowbar he had left on the sand beside me and poked the cut section to see if I could lever it out enough to peer inside.

There was that tremor through the water again, something bounced from my helmet. When I looked up, the wing appeared to move and then, in a kind of slow motion, it dipped and the Heron rolled over to engulf me.

My shoes weighed seventeen and a half pounds each. I had eighty pounds in lead weights strapped around my waist and the brass helmet weighed over fifty pounds. Which explains why I couldn't exactly run for my life.

The most I can say is that all was confusion for a while, sand billowing around me in a great cloud. Something caught me on the right shoulder sending me down on one knee and then I found myself flat on my back.

I lay there for a while, to get my breath back, so-to-speak, then tried to get up which was when I discovered I couldn't move my helmet.

As was to become apparent very quickly, the trailing edge of the starboard wing, digging down into the sand as the plane rolled over, had taken both lifeline and airhose with it, pinning me like a fly on my back.

I lay there for a moment, trying not to panic, aware that air was still getting to me which was, after all, the main thing. All was still confusion, sand swirling around me, then Turk came through it headlong and dropped beside me.

He wasn't smiling this time. He peered in through my face mask to make sure I was still in the land of the living and then moved on to free me. It was round about then that I became aware that water was rising in my suit. I groped at my legs frantically, aware at once of the great gaping tear in my suit on my right thigh.

At the thought of that coldness rising inch by inch into my helmet to choke me, I panicked completely and tugged at Turk's foot. He was with me in a moment and crouched to examine the situation as I pointed.

He moved past me, I felt a tug and found that I could move again, but only a foot or two and when I turned, I saw that both lines were buried irretrievably.

Turk drew his knife, leaned across the wing and sliced through my lifeline then he tied the free end to my harness which didn't make any kind of sense. What happened next was like something out of a nightmare for almost in the same moment, he slashed through the airhose close to my head. And then, as silver bubbles poured out, rising in a linked chain, he followed them up to the surface.

I forced myself to my knees, expecting to inhale water at any moment, but it was still air I breathed, although a distinctly rancid variety. And then with a sudden, fierce tug I was jerked off my feet and hauled to the surface.

When they got the helmet off me, the first thing I was conscious of was the anguish on Sister Claire's face. 'Thank God, Mr Nelson. Thank God.'

Turk shoved a lighted cigarette into my mouth. I said weakly, 'What happened?'

'Well the good Lord didn't save you, that's for sure.'

'What then? You sliced through my hose.'

'Sure I did. The only way to get you free.' He picked up the helmet. 'Most modern helmets have a check valve which closes automatically when the air supply is cut off. The exhaust valve does the same leaving you with what air there is in the suit.'

'And how long is that supposed to last?'

'At the depth you were, perhaps eight minutes. Mind you, that rent in the suit increased the odds some, but what the hell, you made it.'

The cigarette tasted marvellous, so did the glass of rotgut brandy Sister Claire handed me. To my surprise, Turk pulled on his aqualung and adjusted the straps.

I said, 'Now what?'

'Got to see the state of the market, General. No time like the present.'

He went over the side. I sat there for a moment or so longer, just savouring being alive then I asked Sister Claire, who had been hovering anxiously, to help me out of that damned suit.

I was just free of it when Turk surfaced and clambered up the ladder. 'How's it look?' I demanded.

'Fine – the main entrance is clear now. I got inside with no trouble.'

My stomach went hollow. I said, 'Did you see what we came for?'

'You can bet on that. Boxes all over the place. Some of them broken open. One hell of a mess, but nothing we can't handle.' He hesitated and added in a low voice, 'I also found another skeleton.'

He held out his hand and I saw that he

was holding a tarnished silver chain with a religious medal on the end.

'At moments like this I'm strictly a coward,' he said. 'It's all yours, General,' and he turned and went over the side again.

Sister Claire had been aware, I think, that she was the subject of our conversation. She kept on folding the diving suit neatly yet I realised that she was watching me covertly.

Under the circumstances, the best way seemed the direct one so I simply walked up to her and held out the medal. 'Turk found this below. He thought it might mean something to you.'

She examined it for a long moment, then held it to her cheek, the eyes filled with tears. Thank you, Mr Nelson. It belonged to my father. His patron saint. St Martin de Porres.'

She turned and went below.

Sometime later, Turk appeared beside the ladder again carrying a bundle wrapped in layers of heavy sacking. When I took it from him I was surprised to discover how heavy it was.

He climbed up on deck, dripping water and pushed up his mask. 'Thought it looked interesting. How is she?'

I told him, reached for his knife and sliced at the fastening on the bundle. There were several layers of material, carefully stitched together, all of which had to be cut away before the object they concealed could be revealed.

We sat there in silence for a while looking at it and finally, Turk gave a low whistle, 'Now that, my friend, is really quite something. That's where it all hangs out. Do you think it might make her feel better?'

'I don't see why not,' I said.

When we went down to the saloon, Sister Claire sat at the table, her face buried in her hands, the medal dangling between her fingers.

I said softly, 'We've brought you something, Sister.'

She looked up startled and drew in her breath sharply for there on the table in front of her, blackened and tarnished by the water, but still unmistakably one of the most beautiful pieces of art I have seen in my life, was Our Lady of Tizi Benou.

10
The Wild Horsemen

We had something to eat after that, only a light meal for obvious reasons and a short rest. Then we got down to it.

We set up the winch and the portable diesel engine that operated it and Turk instructed Sister Claire in its use. And I ran a signal line on a lead weight out under the rail for her. Two pulls for *Stop*, three for *Haul Away*, which was all she needed to know.

Then we went over the side together and dropped down to the Heron taking the winch line with us, a loading net of stout manilla hemp dangling from the end of the rope.

When I went in through the door to the main cabin, I could see what Turk had meant.

There were boxes jumbled everywhere, some broken open as he had said, ingots spilling out.

What was left of her father was another pathetic, broken skeleton clothed in a few tattered rags. I found a tarpaulin jammed in a corner. We took it between us and covered him over, weighing it down with three or four ingots, though whether they were of gold or silver, I couldn't be sure.

Then we got down to the real work and a back-breaking task it was. As I was told later, we moved just under a ton of gold in all and half a ton of silver plus a box or two of assorted items.

Not all at once, of course, but most of it by the evening of that first day.

Each box took both of us to manhandle it out of the cabin. The loading net could manage four with safety and each time it hoisted to the surface we took turns in going up with it because although Sister Claire could operate the winch she obviously couldn't handle the boxes on her own because of the weight.

Once an hour, we had a complete rest, by which I mean we both went up together and spent the time getting the boxes below where we stacked them neatly in every available spare place from the cabins to the saloon. Our Lady of Tizi Benou was already under the bunk in Sister Claire's cabin wrapped in a blanket.

By early evening I was just about at the end of my tether. My back was aching and my leg was giving me hell and together, I'd just about had it. On top of that the light was beginning to get pretty bad down there and the effects of the constant diving, even at such a shallow depth, were beginning to tell on both of us.

We put another couple of boxes in the net and I don't think either of us could have lifted another one. Turk tapped me on the shoulder and we followed the load up wearily.

I surfaced and found a dugout canoe a yard or two away, a primitive-looking affair with an incongruously modern American outboard motor tacked on at the stern.

I don't know who was more surprised, the

fisherman or wild-fowler or whoever he was who sat in it, or me. He wore a ragged striped shirt, a dirty white burnouse and a straw hat festooned with pieces of string around the brim to keep the mosquitoes away. There were fishing nets in the prow, a couple of dead widgeon and an ancient fowling piece of Moorish design with a barrel a mile long.

As I grabbed for the edge of the canoe, Turk surfaced on the other side, knife in hand. The man cried out in alarm and in the same moment, Sister Claire leaned over the rail.

'No, leave him,' she called. 'He's all right. Just a fisherman from Zarza. Omar, younger brother of the headman. I remember him well. He was very kind to me.'

There was a distinct pause. Turk said, 'Okay, let's have him on board.'

Omar sat cross-legged and smoked the cigarette she gave him smiling anxiously at Turk as we stood there drying ourselves. It was a little chilly now, the frogs were croaking, a sure sign that night could not be far away and on the horizon of things, the sky was the colour of brass.

'You say he remembers you?' Turk asked.

'Once I told him who I was,' she said. 'I've changed remember, but Talif and I were in the village for quite some time.'

'Ask him what he was doing here?'

'I already have. He says he often comes here. It's a good place for wildfowl.'

'Did he know about the plane?'

She spoke to him in quick, fluent Arabic. He replied at some length. She nodded and said, 'Yes, he knew about the plane, has known for about two years now.'

'Then why didn't he tell anybody about it?' I demanded.

'He says it would have brought the authorities in and they like to be left alone.'

Turk said, 'Ask him if he's noticed any other unusual visitors. Another boat perhaps. Anything at all out of the way.'

She spoke to Omar again. 'No one. The tax collector once a year and that was six months ago.'

Turk turned to me. 'All right, General, what do we do with him?'

'God knows. How much longer do you

reckon it should take for us to finish up and get out of here?'

'Noon tomorrow I'd say. Sooner if we get an early start in the morning.'

Omar rattled off at some length to Sister Claire. When he was finished Turk said, 'What was all that about?'

'He wants me to return to the village with him. To see them all.' She put a hand on his shoulder and smiled gently. 'They saved my life. They are a good people.'

'You've got to be joking,' Turk told her. 'Nobody even goes near that village, including our friend here. I'll lock him up in one of the cabins until we're ready to leave.'

'You'll do nothing of the kind, Monsieur.' The only time I knew her to use the French title, but then she was good and mad. 'This man has done us no harm – will do us no harm. I trust him completely. It would be outrageous to treat him in such a way.'

She spoke briefly in Arabic to Omar who went over the rail and dropped into his dugout. A moment later the engine roared into life and he was away.

Turk said, 'You certainly are a woman who likes to have her own way, aren't you, Duchess? Let's hope you're right about our friend out there.'

'I know I am,' she said simply.

As for me, I was suddenly so weary that argument was beyond me. I went below, washed in hot water and shaved, just to make myself feel civilised again. Then I sat at the table in the saloon and drank a large whisky very slowly while Sister Claire prepared a meal.

Even allowing for the fact that it was out of tins she still wasn't much of a cook. It was something to eat, no more than that and afterwards I sat there with another whisky, half asleep.

She went out for a while and returned with the bundle from under her bunk. She unfolded it carefully and set Our Lady of Tizi Benou on the table. It was quite beautiful in spite of the tarnished state of the silver, about two feet in height and superbly proportioned.

Turk rummaged around in one of the lockers under his seat and produced a roll of cotton wadding and a tin can. 'Try that,' he said. 'It's some kind of mild acid. Good for any kind of corrosion or tarnish.'

She went to work; just a small patch at first, but the effect was almost miraculous, the black patina fading away almost instantly, the silver gleaming through.

It really was quite remarkable and when she'd finished, I said, 'I should think they'll be pleased to get her back.'

'Strange, Mr Nelson. You speak of her almost as if she were a real person.'

'Is that bad?' I said. 'She must have been to a great many people. A lot of years since the eleventh century.'

She made no reply, simply sat staring at the image, her hands clasped and I went and lay on my bunk and stared up through the darkness, eyes burning with tiredness. The last thing I seemed to see before I slept was that pale, silvery face and she was smiling at me.

We were at it again by eight o'clock the following morning, a later start than intended, but mainly because Turk and I had slept the sleep of the hard-worked and Sister Claire hadn't bothered to waken us.

Turk wasn't pleased and perhaps because of that, set a killing pace when we went back below. Because of that, what remained in the cabin of the Heron seemed to disappear at an astonishing rate.

We went up together twice to move what had accumulated on deck down below, but it couldn't have been much after ten when we suddenly realised we were down to the last box.

We gave the usual signal, the load started up, Turk moving with it. I don't know why I delayed. It was only momentary anyway, no more than a final glance over my shoulder at the plane.

And then, as I started up, an extraordinary thing happened. A string of horses galloped through the water above my head, legs moving in slow motion.

A moment later a man in a black burnouse and white robes, a rifle slung across his back appeared in a cloud of silver bubbles, hands at Turk's throat. They moved past me in a series of clumsy somersaults and I saw that Turk already had his knife out.

I surfaced briefly to assess the situation and it was immediately apparent that it was about as bad as it could be. There were at least eight of them – quite obviously the Berber horsemen Turk had spoken of. The Husa. The black burnouse and white robes they wore was almost a uniform and they were all armed with rifles.

The horses were fantastic. Dry land, mud, deep water, nothing seemed to stop them. Sister Claire was standing in the stern and one of them vaulted across the rail to join her. I didn't see what happened after that for the simple reason that I had more pressing things to think about.

The horses which just missed landing on top of me had presumably arrived from the reed bed to my rear. Not that it mattered. The only really important point to note was that if I didn't get moving, I stood a fair chance of having my brains kicked out.

As I started to dive, the rider flung himself on my back. It was a silly thing to do because underwater he didn't stand a chance. I kicked hard with my flipper, taking us down and his hands started to slacken. As he broke free, I turned, grabbed at the fluttering robe and held on tight. Then I swam down into deep water.

His burnouse had somehow come free in the struggle and drifted away. His head was shaven, some religious thing I suppose, the face thin and bony, mouth tight shut, eyes starting from their sockets. He glared down at me, kicking frantically as I held on to the robe and then the mouth opened and a moment later, he stopped kicking. When I released him, he drifted away, arms out, turning over and over very slowly.

Turk was down by the Heron. He beckoned and I followed him across the floor of the lagoon to the far side from the boat, finally surfacing among the reeds.

We pushed up our masks and watched what was going on. There were two on deck, several more urging their horses in and out among the reeds in a businesslike way. It was apparent, on closer inspection, that they were nothing like as romantic as they had seemed at first. The black burnouses were shabby things, the robes patched and tattered. Even the rifles weren't much. A couple had MIs, but for the most part they seemed to be armed with old Lee Enfields.

'How many do you make it?' Turk asked softly.

'The ones in the reeds are making a hell of a lot of noise, but I'd say no more than four.'

'Which makes seven with the creeps on deck.'

'So what do we do?' I said.

'There's no way we can take that bunch and you know it. It's what *they* do next that counts.' He frowned, 'What I'd like to know is are they here by chance or design.'

'You mean Sister Claire's good friend Omar let her down?'

'I'd say that was a distinct possibility.'

We didn't talk much after that because proceedings at the boat were much more interesting. They seemed to be having some sort of council of war on deck while the others swam round and round on horseback, an extraordinary sight.

After a while, the anchor was pulled up, but there was no attempt to start the engine. Instead they worked the *Mary Grant* in towards solid ground at the other end of the lagoon. As her prow bit into soft mud, they tossed the anchor out again and the group who had been swimming rode up out of the water and dismounted.

'At least they haven't got around to rape yet,' Turk whispered. 'That's something.'

As he said that, Sister Claire was helped over the rail to firm ground. 'They're treating her with kid gloves,' Turk said. 'Maybe women are in short supply round here.'

I didn't get a chance to reply because a moment later she was in the saddle. Two of the Husa also mounted, one of them took her reins and the three of them disappeared into the reeds.

Which left the other five who tethered their horses and climbed up to the deck of the

Mary Grant. I expected them to start tearing the place apart. Instead they squatted in a circle on deck smoking cigarettes.

'Looks as if they're waiting for something.'

'I shouldn't think so. They can get round to us at their leisure. After all, what harm can we do them?'

'Well how about trying this for size?' Turk said and proceeded to tell me.

I surfaced very gently under the stern and unfastened the straps of my aqualung allowing it to fall away. Turk must have been watching closely from the reeds for his timing was perfect. He burst into the open, floundering about in the shallows minus his aqualung which he had temporarily discarded.

There was pandemonium on deck as everyone crowded to see him and in the confusion, I pulled myself up under the starboard rail and slipped down the companionway.

Somebody fired a shot, but when I peered out of one of the saloon port holes Turk was already back in to the shelter of the reeds and getting his aqualung on again, according to plan.

As I got the cupboard open under the bench and took out the false floor I heard excited cries, the stamping of horses. I rammed a clip into each of the Sterling submachine guns, slung one over my shoulder and went up the companionway cautiously.

Three of the Husa were already halfway across the lagoon, urging their mounts on with shrill cries. The remaining two stood at the rail, rifles ready. As I'd expected, there wasn't a sign of Turk.

I waited until the hunting party had been swallowed up by the reeds, then I moved a little closer and cocked the Sterling with the usual sinister click.

The two gentlemen at the rail turned quickly. I said, 'All right, nice and easy and nobody gets hurt.'

A superfluous observation as they obviously didn't understand a word of English but they knew a submachine gun when they saw one. Knew what it could do at such close quarters.

I made a quick but quite unmistakable gesture and the two rifles went over the side. Then I called, 'All right, Turk, let's be having you.'

Another superfluous remark because he came over the starboard rail at that precise moment.

He shoved up his mask and grinned savagely. 'Now that's what I call team work.'

As he unbuckled his aqualung the hunting party burst out of the reeds, the man in the lead taking off as if he had a five barred gate to cross. I tossed the spare Sterling to Turk who was still disengaging himself and caught it awkwardly.

But for the next thirty seconds I had enough on my hands. One of the men at the rail cried out a warning in Arabic, but he was already too late. I fired one quick burst from the shoulder that lifted the leader back over his horse's rump, was already swinging to catch the second.

God knows how the last one kept his seat on that plunging horse in the confusion, but he did more than that and actually got a shot off from his rifle, firing one-handed and then Turk entered the fray, firing a long, rolling burst that smacked him solidly into the reeds.

There was no following silence for the whole marsh seemed to come alive, birds, thousands of them, rising in confusion to blacken the sky, calling angrily.

The two at the rail waited for death, expecting it, I have no doubt, yet showing not the slightest trace of fear, warriors to the end, which was much as I would have expected.

One of them eased his hand down towards the handle of the knife in his belt and Turk ran forward and rammed the muzzle of the sterling hard up against blackened teeth. 'Watch it!' he said grimly, suddenly a Marine again. He swung the barrel upwards. They raised their hands.

'Now what?' I said.

'God knows. How's your Arabic?'

'About three words.'

'You speak good French, don't you?'

'Only fair.'

'Well, try them, man. Most Algerians I ever

had dealings with understood enough to get by.'

As usual, he was on to something for when I turned to them and said in French, 'The first man to move dies,' there was an immediate reaction.

'Fine, just fine,' Turk said. 'Now tell them to take their clothes off – everything.'

Their reluctance was effectively overcome by a dig in the ribs from the muzzle of a Sterling. Within a couple of minutes they were both naked as the day they were born and standing hands on the rail, feet well back and spread apart.

'Fine,' Turk said. 'Nothing like having his genitals swinging to cool a man down. The Chinese taught us that one in Korea. Now ask them where the other two have taken the Duchess.'

By then they were ready to talk, at least the taller one, an unpleasant-looking specimen with a face half eaten by yaws, was. In fact, once started, he couldn't stop and spoke, as they say, volumes.

It was about as bad as it could be and

Turk, I suspect, knew what I was going to say before I spoke, simply by looking at my face. 'They've taken her to Zarza,' I said. 'They came here on Colonel Taleb's orders, acting on information received.'

'That creep Omar?' He slammed a hand solidly against the bulkhead. 'Jesus, but I knew we should have held on to him. So the whole deal falls to pieces because of her love-thy-neighbour policy.' He stamped about the deck shaking with rage. 'And Taleb – how the hell could he get here in time? It just isn't possible. He was still in Ibiza the night before last.'

'It's fifty-five minutes by air from Ibiza to Barcelona,' I told him. 'You know that and God knows how many flights a day from there to Algiers direct. A two hour flight in a Caravelle, that's all.'

Things were quieter now and the sky was no longer filled with the clamour of the birds. I waited. He said, 'All right, we've got what we came for and we certainly can't help her now. You agree?'

'I shouldn't think we'd stand much of a

chance. He's bound to have troops or police with him. Something like that and there must be more of these characters around.'

'Okay,' he said. 'Let's get out of here and you can tell these two to make a run for it. They can't harm us now.' He went into the wheelhouse and started the engine. The two Husa went over the side with some reluctance, expecting a bullet in the head before they reached the reeds, I suppose, but they didn't get one.

I watched them disappear, then went below and changed into pants and sweater. Strange how cold I felt, but that would be reaction. I swallowed half a glass of brandy and took the bottle with me when I went back on deck.

We were just forcing our way out through the reeds into the original waterway, but when I offered Turk the bottle he waved it away.

'Not now, man,' he said. 'I've got things to do.'

From then on he didn't say a word, working the boat from one channel into another, his face grim and pre-occupied. As on the way in, I stood on top of the wheel-house, checking the route ahead, occasionally warning him of some obstruction.

And then, quite suddenly after half an hour, as we entered a small lagoon, he swung the wheel sharply, boosted the engine and forced the *Mary Grant* into the reeds until we were completely enclosed.

It was very quiet when he switched off the engine and when I jumped down to the deck, I saw he had the sextant out.

'What in the hell are you doing?' I asked him.

'What does it look like, for Christ's sake? I'm checking our position. We've got to have a cross-bearing when we leave the bloody boat otherwise we'll never find it again, will we?'

'That makes sense,' I said slowly.

If I smiled it was unconsciously. He said, 'What's so funny? So we're turning our backs on two and half million dollars and going to get our throats cut instead and for what?'

'The most infuriating woman I've ever met in my life,' I told him.

'In spades, General, in spades. Now get the inflatable out and let's get moving.'

One thing about the inflatable – it would go just about anywhere, certainly through areas impassable to the *Mary Grant* and with the outboard motor we made good time.

We were well armed, of course. A Browning apiece and the Sterlings although I'd rather have had an AK assault rifle or an M16 any day. But whichever way you looked at it, it was a reasonably foolhardy enterprise.

We hadn't the slightest inkling of what waited for us, no idea of what we were going to do when we got there anyway. One thing did puzzle me. The fact that Taleb had left it all to the Husa. All right, the fact that they knew their way around the marshes, spoke for itself. That was rather like the cavalry in the old days using Indian trackers, but I would have thought he could have called in a helicopter.

Turk had spent most of his time sitting in

the prow with a chart and that compass on the string about his neck and finally he turned and told me to kill the motor.

'By my reckoning we're about half a mile out,' he said. 'From now on we paddle.'

Which made sense, even allowing for the fact that other fishermen, like Omar, used outboards on their canoes.

It was close to noon now, the sun high in the sky and the heat was intense. And so was the silence. Not a bird called anywhere, nothing seemed disturbed at our passing. Only the quiet splash of the paddles dipping in and out.

A handful of wild duck lifted in alarm from the reeds up ahead on the right. I should have realised, recognised at once what it meant, but I was half asleep in that stifling heat and it took time for it to sink in.

Turk turned to say something, there was a single shot, his hands went to his face as he cried out, blood spurting between his fingers. He went over the side backwards as I grabbed for him, catching him by the belt.

And then another shot ripped through the

inflatable followed by that high, clear Husa cry as they charged out of the reeds, half a dozen of them.

The inflatable was already sinking. Turk went one way and I another. I caught a final glimpse of him, the face a mass of scarlet and then he slipped beneath the surface.

A moment later I went down under trampling hooves.

11
Zarza

I came into Zarza more dead than alive at the tail end of a horse, hands lashed behind my back, a rope around my neck. When I couldn't walk they dragged me, it was as simple as that, a remarkable incentive to stay on one's feet.

It wasn't much of a place. About what I'd expected. A couple of dozen thatched huts fighting each other for room on a small island at one end of a broad, shallow lagoon. In fact land was in such short supply that some of the huts were built out over the water on stilts.

There was a rickety jetty, a few canoes and nothing else. And I mean nothing. Not a single human being in sight or so I thought until they dragged me up on dry land and I realised that what I had imagined to be a bundle of rags hanging between two poles was, in fact, friend Omar or what was left of him.

They tethered their horses in a bunch to one of the poles, tied my neck rope to the other and left me with my face in the dirt after a friendly kick in the ribs.

The house they went into was larger than the others, presumably the headman's, and after a while, there seemed to be something of a disturbance in there.

A woman ran out, whether young or old it was impossible to say at that distance although, for a heart-stopping moment, I thought it might be Sister Claire. She didn't get very far before the Husa who erupted from the door behind her ran her down, laughing like a madman. Two or three others appeared on the porch, shouting advice as he struggled with the woman. They looked good and drunk to me so obviously this was their day for disregarding the Koran.

Finally the one with the woman decided he'd had enough and hit her with his clenched fist. Then he caught her over his shoulder and walked back to the house. The others got out of the way to let him through, laughing heartily and then followed him in.

One of them changed his mind at the last moment, came down the steps and staggered towards the horses. He examined one, obviously his own, speaking to it in Arabic, fondling its ears, then he looked up at Omar, raising the bottle in his right hand in a kind of toast.

He turned his attention to me. A preliminary kick in the ribs to bring me back to life, then he crouched down, forced open my mouth and poured some of the contents of the bottle into it. Which wasn't such a bad idea in the circumstances only he went on too long and I nearly choked. Finally, he urinated on me with great care, not wasting a drop and staggered back to the house, singing cheerfully.

Incredibly, Omar suddenly made some sort of movement. When I glanced up, he was trying to look down at me, but he didn't seem to see the funny side of things at all.

Neither did I.

I suppose I must have lain there for an hour and there was still no sign of any of the inhabitants whom, I presumed, had been ordered to stay indoors for I couldn't imagine that even the Husa would have killed the lot of them.

Finally, Omar gave a dreadful groan, his body shook convulsively and he went very still. The conclusion was obvious and then I heard the sound of an engine and a launch appeared from the marsh and started across the lagoon.

It was a shabby old thirty-footer and badly needed a fresh coat of paint. It flew the Algerian flag, there was a Browning heavy machine gun mounted in the prow, two or three of those on deck were in khaki uniforms, but on the whole, it seemed a strangely down-at-heel affair for a government boat.

The two Husa we'd sent naked into the

world stood by the port rail. Someone had given them each a pair of cellular underpants to wear. At any other time, their appearance could have induced a mild hysteria in me, but not now.

When the launch tied up at the ramshackle old jetty the first person ashore was Taleb. He was in uniform and wore one of those Africa Corps caps, khaki slacks and bush shirt, two rows of medal ribbons above his left pocket. There was a Browning in the holster on his hip.

A couple of the men who'd brought me in came down from the house and spoke to him. He listened to what they had to say and when he walked towards me he was followed by another army officer. A captain this one. A small, shabby man with a pock-marked face and crumpled uniform. He stayed a respectful pace or two behind Taleb and the two Husa in their underpants lurked at his heels like a couple of underfed dogs.

When they were close enough, they couldn't hold themselves in any longer and tried to get at me, coming in with a rush. Taleb shouted angrily, moved in quickly and started to beat them about the head with the leather swagger stick he carried in one hand.

He squatted beside me and lit a cigarette. 'You can't blame them, Mr Nelson. You've killed several of their friends, after all. So, your friend Turkovich is dead?'

All I wanted to do was spit at him, but my mouth was too dry.

He chuckled and tapped me on the cheek with the swagger stick. 'Never mind. You'll feel better after a bath and a drink then we'll talk again, eh? I'll get Captain Husseini here to see to it.'

He spoke briefly to Husseini then went up to the headman's house. A couple of soldiers had joined Husseini from the boat and in response to his orders, one of them got a bucket of water from the lagoon and sluiced me down which was presumably meant to be the bath Taleb had referred to.

Then the neck rope was removed and my hands untied. I stood up flexing my wrists and Husseini gave me a shove towards the headman's house. As we approached, several drunken Husa rushed out, heads down, Taleb driving them before him.

He stood at the top of the steps looking down at me, anonymous behind the dark glasses he wore against the sun and then he smiled. 'Children, Mr Nelson. Stupid and barbaric, but they have their uses.' He pointed towards Omar 'They're really very good at that sort of work.'

'Obviously.'

'But now we must see about that drink I promised you,' and he turned and led the way inside.

It was as primitive as one would have expected. No tables or chairs or anything exotic like that. It was obviously the sort of place where people wrapped themselves in a blanket at night and slept in the corner.

On the whole, the furniture consisted of a few tattered rugs. Taleb sat on a wooden box against the wall. To one side of him was a doorway into another room masked by a rush curtain to keep out the flies as was the front door.

He said something to Husseini who produced a bottle and two glasses with alacrity.

'You'll join me?' Taleb asked.

The way I felt I hadn't any intention of saying no. 'Why not?'

I took one of the glasses. It was neat gin, hardly one of my favourites, but better than nothing. Husseini hovered on the fringe of things, eager to please. He was obviously disappointed when Taleb dismissed him and he retired like a hurt dog to a position by the door.

Taleb said, 'He would make an excellent valet, Husseini, so eager to please. He has not, I regret to say, enjoyed the most successful of military careers.'

'Doesn't he mind having himself dissected in public?'

'He doesn't understand a word of English, my friend, which means that you and I can get down to more serious matters without any kind of interruption.'

'What about Sister Claire?'

'Later,' he said firmly. 'For the moment, she is quite safe, but we have more important matters to discuss. When my Husa friends took me to this place where they'd left the boat all we found were dead men.'

'Very sorry, but they did rather bungle the whole business, you must admit.'

'Gladly.' He leaned forward to top up my glass. 'So you've moved the boat to another location, which also means that you have managed to raise most of the gold. The Bouvier woman wasn't very forthcoming, but the two men who brought her in said the cabins were full of boxes.'

I said, 'One thing puzzles me. How in the hell you turned up here so fast.'

'No great trick, Mr Nelson.' He shrugged. 'I was in Algiers by noon the day before yesterday. In fact, I was at the mouth of the Khufra estuary waiting for you on the night you came in.'

'Only we didn't come. That must have worried you.'

'You came in the back way? Very

commendable. I knew it was possible of course, but I was told it was a lengthy and rather unpleasant process.'

He took a cigarette from a silver case and placed it carefully between his lips. Husseini rushed in with an ugly brass lighter that flared like a petrol bomb.

Taleb said, 'Let's get down to brass tacks, as you English say. You moved the launch, which makes sense and you must have plotted its position very carefully before leaving which makes even more sense, otherwise you could never hope to find it again in this wilderness.'

The gin was making me feel worse instead of better. I put down my glass and said. 'All right. What are you offering?'

He frowned. 'My dear Mr Nelson, I don't need to offer you anything.'

I moved to the window and looked out at the launch. 'Is that really the best that the Algerian Army can do?'

'I don't follow you,' he said warily.

'Don't you.' I turned to face him. 'Well let me spell it out for you. I knew there was something wrong from the start. Not a navy boat in sight in the coastal area, not even a helicopter out looking for us in the marshes. It didn't make sense.'

He sat staring up at me, the eyes very blue in the dark face. I said, 'But everything else does. The shabby, broken-down launch, the third rate officer with a handful of soldiers who's only too anxious to please the great Colonel Taleb. And the Husa to do your throat cutting for a few packets of cigarettes.'

'What are you suggesting, Mr Nelson?' he said calmly.

'That you want the whole bloody lot for yourself.'

He stood up and went to the window and looked outside for a long moment. When he turned, his face had changed slightly. It's difficult to put it into words. He was still calm and yet there was an edge to things.

'Just now, Mr Nelson, you referred to me as the great Colonel Taleb. There is a certain truth in this. I have considerable power, all security men have the world over. I am trusted by those in high places.'

'So what's your beef?' I demanded.

'Blue eyes, my friend.' Here he tapped a finger to his temple. 'Blue eyes in a brown face.'

For a wild moment I thought he'd gone mad. 'What in the hell are you talking about?'

'Mr Nelson, I lived a life of great danger for many years. I fought with the F.L.N. against the French, did everything a man could do to help free his country, spilled my own blood in its soil.'

Which was putting it dramatically, but by now, he was obviously feeling pretty emotional. 'All this, Mr Nelson. All this agony and sweat over the years, but not by one iota does it wipe out my blue eyes or erase the memory of my French mother. I am *chi-chi*. Half-and-half and they never let me forget it.'

He turned to the window as if overcome by emotion. After a while he seemed to get some sort of control and turned to face me again. 'You ask me do I want what you found in that plane for myself. The answer is obvious. I want payment for all those lost years and I want out.'

I laughed in his face. 'What was it you said to me in Ibiza? Something about the French having squeezed this country dry. Something about that gold belonging to the people of Algeria?'

'Am I any worse than you, my friend? Do you think I don't know that you and Turkovich intended to cut yourselves in for a very large slice of the cake?' He raised his voice. 'Or didn't you know that, my dear Sister?'

He said something in Arabic and Sister Claire was pushed in through the curtain by a soldier with a rifle over his shoulder.

She came close and looked up at me, her face calm as I had ever seen it, yet there was real anxiety in the eyes. 'He told me that Mr Turkovich is dead? Is it true?'

'I'm afraid so.'

'Dear God.' She closed her eyes and crossed herself.

Taleb said, 'I asked you a question, woman.'

'A question.' She turned to face him a trifle impatiently. 'Of course I knew what

Mr Nelson and his friend intended. Knew from the beginning.'

A look of astonishment appeared on his face for as always one tended to believe her. 'Did you know about Talif? Did he tell you that?'

She swung to face me, her eyes widening. 'What about Talif? What does he mean?'

I couldn't think of a thing to say and she turned from me, shoulders sagging, the life going out of her.

Taleb stood up again. 'Yes, Sister, a costly little operation so far if measured in human lives.' He turned to me and added briskly, 'I've really been more than kind, Mr Nelson, but there are many things about you I admire, so I'm going to make you a very fair offer. Twenty per cent.'

'You've got nerve, I'll give you that,' I said.

But Sister Claire cut in sharply. 'Mr Nelson,' she said, 'don't you dare. Do you hear me?' She ran forward and gripped my arms painfully above the elbows.

My leg hurt, the gin hadn't mixed too well with all that swamp water in my stomach, and frankly, Taleb's offer in the circumstances, was pretty staggering.

I took a deep breath, turned to him and said, 'Go to hell.'

He wasn't in the least put out. 'Very well then, this is how it will be. I give you half an hour to talk things over together. Half an hour to decide to be sensible. At the end of that time, you can go free, Mr Nelson, because I admire a man of courage and fortitude. I'll send you into Algiers and arrange for you to be transported back to Ibiza.'

It didn't make any kind of sense and I said, 'And Sister Claire?'

'Goes to the Husa. The choice is yours.'

He said something in Arabic to Husseini and left quickly before I could even begin to argue.

Husseini called a guard, a small, wizened man in a uniform two sizes too large for him who carried his old-fashioned rifle at the slope. At first I thought he was going to leave us where we were until he beckoned and led the way outside.

There was a hut perhaps twenty or thirty yards out from the lagoon constructed entirely on a foundation of wood pilings which supported it a couple of feet above the surface of the lagoon. It was reached by a long and rickety catwalk and Husseini obviously chose it for security reasons.

He kicked open the door and we went inside. From the looks of it, it was used as a storeroom more than anything else. Fishing nets were draped from the ceiling, there was an old canoe against one wall and the wood floor was broken and uneven, the surface of the lagoon gleaming through the gaps between the planks.

Husseini produced a packet of cigarettes, put one in my mouth, his face serious. The brass petrol lighter flared momentarily then he withdrew without a word. We could see him clearly through the screen door as he spoke to the sentry, then walked away along the swaying catwalk.

I said, 'What's called a tricky situation.'

'Please, Mr Nelson, we haven't got much time and there are many things I need to know.'

'Such as?'

'What exactly happened to you and Mr Turkovich after the Husa took me away from the boat?'

I told her briefly. When I was finished, she said in an irritatingly detached way, 'I shall pray for him.'

The anger was something I found difficult to contain. I said, with some violence, 'He could have been well out to sea by now, Sister, home and away. We both could.'

She looked at me with a slight frown, as if not really understanding what I was getting at. I see now that I was simply wasting my time for she saw nothing special in what we had done – nothing extraordinary. It was all simply part of the natural order of things.

She said, 'Tell me about Talif, Mr Nelson, and don't try to spare me this time.'

'All right,' I said. 'I found him in the well at that old farm he was using. When I went to get water for the jeep. He'd been murdered.'

'Why didn't you tell me?'

'You'd have gone to the police, wouldn't you?'

She nodded slowly. 'Yes, that's true. I don't suppose I would have had any other choice.'

'Which would have knocked everything on the head in no uncertain manner.'

She looked at me in a strangely detached way, through and beyond, if you follow me. 'Ah, I see now. You had already decided at that point that you wished to . . .' Here she hesitated. 'Help me, is that how we should put it? How much did you intend to leave me?'

'Half,' I said.

'I see.'

She sat there nodding to herself reflectively and I exploded again. 'For God's sake, take a good look at yourself for a change instead of stripping other people to the bone. I lost my plane, my livelihood because I helped you. Did you ever even mention compensation once?'

She seemed surprised. 'But we had a contract. You accepted the terms. The money is needed elsewhere. Really needed. I thought you understood that.'

The feeling of utter frustration was fantastic. 'Look, what did you ever offer Turk and me? A handful of loose change compared to the real size of the pot and in exchange, we were expected to go through hell and high water.'

'We made a bargain, Mr Nelson,' she said stubbornly. 'The terms were agreed – mutually agreed. I expect you to abide by them.'

She was talking as though everything was still turning over according to plan. It really was quite astounding. I stared at her in astonishment, unable to think of a single damn thing to say.

There was a light, but distinctive tapping against the floor and a familiar, if slightly hoarse, voice said, 'Heh, General, do you think there's a chance that you two could shut up long enough for me to get a word in?' I lay on my stomach and peered down through a crack between the planks at Turk who hung onto one of the pilings, his face barely above water. His forehead was terribly bruised, flesh gouged out almost bone-deep in a strip that disappeared into the hair.

Sister Claire knelt beside me, her face shining. 'Mr Turkovich,' she said softly. 'Is it you?'

'In the flesh and twice as handsome, Duchess.'

'I thought you'd had it,' I said. 'What happened?'

'Oh, the bastards can't shoot straight. I've been watching from the reeds for an hour. Saw them bring you here. What's the score?'

I told him quickly enough. When I was finished he said, 'Okay, so we'd better get you out of here and fast. Are you game to make a run for it, Duchess?'

'I'd rather take my chances with the Khufra than Colonel Taleb,' she whispered.

'Okay, get ready to go.'

He disappeared beneath the surface, sounded again under the catwalk. I turned to the door, crouching on one knee, saw a hand come over the edge of the catwalk and grab for the sentry's ankle. He went over the edge with a cry of alarm.

I didn't wait to see if anyone had been alerted. Simply got the door open fast, pulling Sister Claire out behind me. I shoved her over the edge into the water and dropped in beside her, aware of the commotion under the catwalk where Turk was dealing with the soldier.

We swam out from under the hut and started for the reeds which at that point were the best part of a hundred yards away on the other side of the lagoon. Turk caught up with us before we had gone twenty yards.

'Halfway across it gets shallow enough to wade at this point,' he said. 'So get ready to run.'

I heard a startled cry and turned to see Captain Husseini at the end of the catwalk. He turned and ran along the shore very fast, grabbed the nearest dugout and shoved it out into the water.

We redoubled our efforts and a few moments later, my knees scratched against sand. As I stood up, I glanced over my shoulder. Taleb had just appeared on the deck of the launch and several Husa were running to the water's edge.

Husseini seemed to be having trouble with the outboard motor on the dugout he had chosen but suddenly it roared into life and the boat shot out into the lagoon.

He drew his pistol and fired a single shot which must have been at least twenty yards wide of the mark, but it kept us on the move wonderfully, Turk and I dragging Sister Claire between us and as he fired again, we plunged into the safety of the reeds.

The water deepened after a few yards and we floundered on desperately, the outboard motor uncomfortably loud now. A little further on and we came to the edge of another wide, shallow lagoon.

We paused in the shelter of the reeds. Turk said, 'We'd never make it across before he got to us.'

Which was true enough because a second later, the dugout shot out of the entrance to a narrow waterway no more than twenty or thirty yards to the right and started along the edge of the lagoon.

'Call him, Duchess,' Turk said and as she turned to him in astonishment, he shoved her out into the open. 'Go on, for Christ's sake. Scream – anything you like, only get him here.'

There was no need, for Husseini, attracted by the noise, had already turned in a tight circle and was coming back. He cut the motor, the dugout drifting lazily and leaned forward, his pistol ready as Sister Claire floundered towards him.

Turk faded beneath the surface, to reappear a moment later behind the good captain who went back over the side before he knew what hit him. I flung myself forward, catching at the dugout to prevent it capsizing.

Husseini surfaced, found his feet and lurched into me. I grabbed him by the front of the tunic, fist raised to strike and then, for some inconsequential reason, remembered the cigarette.

I shoved him away. 'Go on, get out of it!' I yelled and although I'd spoken in English, he obviously got the drift for he turned and plunged into the reeds.

Turk was holding the dugout as Sister Claire clambered in. I did the same for him and joined them. 'Now what?' I said.

With a quick jerk, he snapped the string around his neck and gave me the compass then he took something from inside his shirt and passed it across. It was the Khufra chart, soaked so badly that in places it was coming adrift but still legible.

'I'd say we were still in the game, wouldn't you?' He pulled the starter cord and the outboard roared into life. 'Now let's get the hell out of here.'

I could hear the Husa calling to each other, a great deal of confused shouting and the launch's engines started up, but by then it was too late. We moved on into the marsh rapidly, turning from one waterway into another and all sounds faded.

12

A Sound of Thunder

It took us an hour and a half to get back to the boat and when I clambered over the rail, it was something of a relief to feel the deck beneath my feet again. I turned to help Sister Claire and Turk clambered up behind her.

We were all close to the point of exhaustion so much was obvious, but Turk looked particularly bad, his face paler than I had ever seen it, eyes glittering, that great, swollen gash oozing blood.

He leaned against the wheelhouse and I said anxiously, 'Are you all right?'

'Nothing a drink won't cure.'

'Nonsense, Mr Turkovich. You could well

be suffering from concussion. Alcohol could be very bad for you,' Sister Claire told him.

. He gave her a tired smile. 'People have been telling me that all my life, Duchess. Why should I start listening now?' He went down the companionway and she followed, still protesting. I climbed up on top of the wheelhouse, with some difficulty, I might add, and had a look at the general situation. All seemed quiet so I went below.

Obviously they had decided on a compromise for although Turk had a glass of brandy in his hand, he was allowing her to do what she could for his wound. She very obviously knew her job and was helped by the fact that Turk's medical kit was of the type used by the U.S. navy on active service which meant that it included just about everything that could possibly be needed in any situation short of a major operation.

I went into the galley and made some coffee and when I took it out into the saloon, she was just finishing taping a bandage around his head. He kissed her hand extravagantly,

'The Lady with the Lamp, I always knew it
– or wasn't she with the other lot?'

She actually smiled, really smiled, yet when
she slumped down on to one of the benches
she looked so tired, all energy draining out
of her that I thought she might pass out.

She took the coffee I offered her gratefully
and sat there, nursing the cup in both hands
as if appreciating the warmth. 'You are very
kind – both of you.'

'You mean under the circumstances, don't
you?' I said bitterly.

Turk frowned. 'What is this? What's going
on?'

'She knows,' I said and reached for the
brandy bottle.

'Knows what, man?'

I looked up at her. 'How would you
describe it, Sister? That we're going to steal
half your money.'

'No, Mr Nelson, not mine,' she said quietly.
'That is something you never seem to have
realised from the beginning. Not mine to give
and certainly not yours to take. You asked
me once how much the contents of these

boxes were worth, Mr Nelson. You tell me. One thousand lives saved? Ten thousand?'

Suddenly I couldn't bear to look her in the face. Not because of any sense of shame or anything like that. It was just that I'd had enough.

'Why don't you get off my back?' I said. 'I'm tired of being St Christopher. Try somebody else. Try him.'

Turk smiled wanly. 'Not me, Duchess. All I can do to carry myself these days.'

She went out. Her cabin door closed. Turk reached across and poured a little more brandy into my glass. 'Don't let her get to you, General. If she took you to court – any court – they'd still award you more than she's willing to pay.'

'I've just never known anybody quite like her,' I said. 'She's so bloody unreasonable.'

He yawned. 'They always are, aren't they?'

'What are you talking about?'

'The forsake-all-others-and-cling-only-unto-me type. They see the truth so there's no room for any deviation.'

'The truth as they see it, you mean?'

'That's what I said, General.' He yawned again. 'Christ, I'm bushed.'

He pillowed his head on his arms. I sat there thinking about it. Tried closing my eyes myself for a while, but they were hot and burning and refused to stay shut so I went up on deck.

The sky was grey and overcast and it was still quiet in the heat of the afternoon, the occasional flutter of a bird in the reeds, no more than that. And then very faintly in the distance I heard the Husa calling to each other.

I went into the wheelhouse and got the field glasses then I climbed up on top again and peered out through the camouflage net. I could hear them quite distinctly now, but I couldn't see a thing and at one point I thought I heard the launch also.

It was so still in that great heat that it was difficult to judge sound and distance. As I turned away, something quite unexpected happened. It started to rain, great, heavy swollen drops splashing through the camouflage net. Within seconds it had increased into a torrential downpour.

I hurried below and shook Turk awake. He looked up at me stupidly. 'What's going on?'

'It's raining,' I said. 'The monsoon couldn't do better and I could hear the Husa – somewhere out there.'

'Anything else?'

'Thought I heard the launch, but I'm not as certain about that.'

Sister Claire emerged from the cabin in time to hear this last remark. 'Trouble?' she enquired.

'Nothing we can't handle,' Turk told her. 'Let's have the chart out here, General.'

I unfolded it gingerly and Turk leaned over it. 'If we go out the way we came in, we'll be mucking about for hours and this rain will make things a hell of a sight worse.'

'What are you suggesting?'

'From here to the Khufra estuary is a clear run. Half an hour at the most and straight out to sea through the narrows. If we move fast enough we'll be to hell and gone while Taleb and his boys are still combing the marshes for us. What do you think?'

It made sense, every kind of sense, to make

a run for it before the opposition realised what was happening and the rain would help rather than hinder, providing the right kind of dirty weather for the run out to sea.

'Sounds fine to me,' I said.

'Then what are we waiting for?'

Turk throttled back until the engine was little more than a low murmur, but we still made good time in spite of the fact that the rain, by now, was so heavy that visibility was reduced to a few yards.

Sister Claire had stayed below. It was a difficult situation now, to put it mildly and I suggested as much to Turk.

'For God's sake,' he said. 'She wouldn't even be here if it wasn't for us. We went back for her didn't we?'

Which was true enough and in any case there were more important things to think of at the moment. I busied myself at the chart checking the course thoroughly.

'How's it look?' he asked me when I'd finished.

'Straight up and down as long as you're right about the estuary. You'd better be. We wouldn't last very long in a punch up. We've nothing left to fight with.'

'That's what you think,' he said. 'Run your hand under the chart table.'

I did as he suggested and found a revolver secured by a metal clip, a Smith and Wesson .38, fully loaded. 'Is this all?'

'Two seconds ago you had nothing. Don't knock it, General. It's loaded with magnum bullets and there's a box of them in the drawer under the charts. One of those babies will stop a car engine.'

'And which sales pamphlet did you read that in?'

'Stick with me,' he said. 'We're going to make it, I promise you. You'll live for ever and die rich. Now take over the wheel. I want to go below.'

In spite of his apparent good spirits, he seemed tired and he certainly looked terrible. Strange, but as I stood there alone at the wheel in the mist and rain I was reminded of him as he had been when I'd first met him.

So extraordinarily self-contained, so sure of himself, so much his own man or had all that quite simply been an illusion?

The door opened and Sister Claire came in. She was wearing the sou'wester and yellow oilskin again against the rain and carried a tray covered with a cloth. There was coffee underneath and sandwiches.

'Just what the doctor ordered,' I said brightly.

But she didn't respond and looked out of the window into the rain. 'Is it far now to the estuary?'

'Ten or fifteen minutes, that's all. Where's Turk?'

'In his cabin. The door was open as I went by. He was having a fix.'

She didn't sound exactly enthusiastic so I said, 'If it keeps him going, then that's all right. You said something like that yourself when we started out. I'd say he's done rather well under the circumstances.'

'Undoubtedly,' she said. 'You both have.'

'Only we've disappointed you?'

She went out, brushing past Turk without

a word as he entered. 'From the look on your face I can see you've been having another heart-to-heart with St Joan.'

'Something like that.'

He was full of himself, colour in his cheeks again, and reached for a sandwich. 'What's in these?'

'Tinned ham.'

He bit into one and leaned over the chart and quite suddenly the narrow waterway we were in widened and we passed out into the main stream of the Khufra.

There was quite a current running and the wheel bucked in my hands. Turk said, 'The estuary is about half a mile from here according to this so just cool it a little until we've had a chance to see the state of the nation.'

The rain still hammered down, the turbulent water in the centre of the stream slapped against the hull of the *Mary Grant* with a hollow booming sound.

Sister Claire came back on deck and joined us. 'What's happening? Are we there?'

'Any minute now, Duchess,' Turk told her. 'Any minute now.'

And then the curtain of rain seemed to be pushed aside as by an invisible hand and we could see the whole of the estuary area, a desolate enough looking place with the reed banks crowding in on either side of the river and sandbanks ridging the water everywhere leaving only the one clear channel to the sea.

We were the only living things on view, that was the important thing and Turk gave vent to a high rebel yell. 'What did I tell you, General? Home and dry. Here, give me that wheel.'

He pushed me out of the way, grabbed the wheel and went up to full power, laughing like a crazy man, the bows lifting out of the turbulent water.

The Browning .30 machine gun has a range of at least two miles and fires around eight high velocity bullets every second and it can't fire single shots.

The first burst caught us somewhere near the prow and the *Mary Grant* lurched wildly to one side, Turk lost control of the wheel, Sister Claire was thrown to the floor and he fell on top of her.

I went down on one knee which was just as well because it meant we were all at floor level when the second burst knocked out every window in the wheelhouse, showering us with glass and splintered wood.

Taleb's shabby old launch surged out of the reeds on the far side of the stream between us and the outlet, a couple of soldiers crouched behind the Browning. As they fired another burst that ripped into the hull and starboard deck, I got to my feet, gave the engines everything they had and spun the wheel to port.

The Browning chattered again, chipping wood from the wheelhouse panelling to one side and a sudden, violent blow in the left arm pushed me forward over the wheel.

And then we hit the reed wall with the force of a battering ram, it parted before us and swallowed the *Mary Grant* whole.

I had obviously passed out for a while, only a minute or so, but when I came to, I was squatting in the corner and Sister Claire had the medical kit open and was tearing off my shirt sleeve.

A gunshot wound seldom hurts at first, the shock to the central nervous system is too great. Pain comes later, but for the moment, my left arm was simply numb. I could even move the fingers and only a pair of rather obscene looking purple lips on each side of the bicep indicated that a bullet had passed straight through.

She cleaned it up quickly and clapped a field dressing over it. Turk was standing up, the Smith and Wesson in his hand, peering out through the shattered windows.

'What's happening?' I said.

'The bastards are just cruising up and down for the moment.'

Sister Claire broke open a morphine ampoule and stuck it in my arm. 'If it starts to hurt let me know and I'll give you another.'

I thanked her and got to my feet. 'Why doesn't he come straight in after us?'

'I think that the moment we try and clear off through the reeds he will. He's just biding his time, waiting for us to make the first move. Another thing, he doesn't know whether we're carrying any hardware or not.'

Which was a point. I said, 'All right, we'd better take a look.'

We clambered up on top of the wheelhouse and peered cautiously over the top of the reeds in time to see the launch crossing the estuary towards us at full speed. The Browning chattered again, scything through the reeds, hammering into the hull of the *Mary Grant*.

At the last moment, it swerved sharply, heeling over to starboard, a great wave washing through the reeds, exposing the whole length of the boat to us at a range of no more than thirty yards.

Turk seized his opportunity and stood up straight. Holding the Smith and Wesson out in front of him in both hands. He fired three times at the two soldiers behind the Browning knocking one of them over the rail into the water and put the other three rounds through the wheelhouse.

There was a sudden cry, the launch veered away sharply and he dropped back out of sight and ejected the empty shells.

'That'll give the bastard something to think about.' He started to reload, with the handful of rounds he'd crammed into his pocket.

But not for long. We were on borrowed time, that much was certain. The launch came in again, even faster, fired a long sustained burst which luckily wasn't even on target, slicing through the reeds to one side of us. This time she swerved away when she was still sixty or seventy yards out and although Turk tried to repeat his previous performance, the most he managed to do was clip the hull in a couple of places.

The launch shot away into the rain and disappeared. We dropped down to the deck again and he started to reload.

I said, 'How long does it go on? We only need one really good burst in the right place and we'll go up like a bomb.'

'Don't rub it in,' Turk said. 'Last time I buy a boat with petrol engines.'

Sister Claire had blood on one cheek from a flying splinter, but didn't seem to have noticed. She said, 'We can't surrender – we can't!'

'The Church militant,' Turk said. 'Now I believe that bishops rode into battle armed with maces in the Middle Ages. What would you like us to do, Duchess? Go out and die like men?'

A great hollow voice boomed out of the rain. 'Nelson? Are you there?'

'Loud-hailer,' Turk said. 'Seems he wants to talk. We don't have one, by the way, so you'll just have to use your lungs.'

I climbed up on top of the wheelhouse and peered out over the reeds. The launch lay almost in midstream just visible, but shrouded by the rain. When I looked through the field glasses I couldn't see any sign of Taleb, who was presumably inside the wheelhouse.

I cupped my hands and yelled, 'What do you want?'

His boice boomed back like an echo. 'This is stupid. Nothing to be gained, Nelson. Let's behave like sensible men. Let's talk.'

'Which means a bullet in the back of the skull at the first opportunity,' I said to Turk who was standing on deck at the side of the wheelhouse with Sister Claire.

He seemed unnaturally excited and my first thought was that he was burning up with fever from his wound or had perhaps over-dosed. But it proved to be neither of these things.

'Tell him you'll go across,' he said urgently. 'There's a spare outboard and another inflat-able in the hold. We can blow it up quickly enough with one of the air bottles.'

'What in the hell are you getting at?' I demanded.

'It's easy, General,' he said. 'I'll go over with you, only under the surface. While you have a nice serious chat with our Algerian friend, I'll stick a lump of that AR17 plastic explosive I showed you to the keel. Add one of those chemical fuses and I guarantee that baby will go down like a stone.'

'And what if he decides to hang on to me?' I demanded. 'What if the whole thing's a come on?'

'Then you lose, General, and we win.' He smiled, managing to look closer to the Devil himself than I would have thought possible.

Sister Claire didn't smile. She suddenly

looked desperate, stricken by the enormity of the whole thing, suddenly out of her depth, unable to cope.

She clutched at Turk's arm. 'No, please, no more killing. No more.'

'All right, Duchess,' he said calmly. 'You tell me. What's your alternative? Shall we offer to give him the lot, do you think that will do?' He shook his head. 'I've got news for you. One way or the other, we end up at the bottom of the bay. Our good friend Taleb has too tidy a mind to have it any other way.'

She stared up at him, her eyes very dark and full of pain and then her shoulders sagged, her head went down.

'Sorry, Duchess,' he said. 'That's the way the world turns.' He nodded to me. 'Okay, give him the good word and let's get on with it.'

I had to push the outboard up to full power to fight the current on the way across, which made me wonder how Turk was managing. On the other hand, nobody knew his business better than he did. If anybody could do it, it was him.

As I came close to the launch, the evidence of Turk's marksmanship was plain. There were four holes in the hull above the watermark that I could see and one of the wheelhouse windows was shattered.

A couple of soldiers were at the rail, one of them clutching a rifle, the other a line and Husseini stood behind them. I was sorry about that in a detached sort of way, though as the Arab would say, it only proved how impossible it was for a man to evade his fate.

As I cut the motor and drifted in, one of the soldiers tossed me a line. I caught it and tied up quickly and they dropped a ladder over the side.

When I went over the rail, Husseini was waiting. He gazed at me reproachfully then made a pretty obvious sign which sent my hands above my heads while he searched me, rather clumsily, for concealed weapons.

Satisfied, he turned and led the way along the deck to the companionway, standing to one side to let me go down first.

When I went into the saloon Taleb was sitting at the table drinking coffee and reading a magazine. I suppose it was all meant to impress on me the undeniable fact that he was top dog and that was all there was to it.

He didn't ask me to sit down. Simply looked at me speculatively. 'I'm not going to waste any more time, Nelson. This is my last offer. You and your friend can keep a hundred thousand for yourselves and be on your way, free men, within half an hour.'

'And Sister Claire?'

He was genuinely angry for the first time since I'd known him. 'If you want to put a few coins in the poor box that's your affair, but otherwise she gets nothing. Now what do you say?'

'I'll have to talk it over with Turkovich.'

'Naturally, I accept that.' He glanced at his watch. 'I'll give you fifteen minutes to make up your mind.'

I said, 'That hardly gives me enough time to get back.'

'Then you'd better get moving, hadn't

you?' he observed. 'Fifteen minutes, Nelson, then I come in, guns blazing.'

'You'll blow us sky high if you do and lose everything,' I said. 'We've got petrol engines.'

'I'll take that chance.'

He poured himself some more coffee, dismissing me and I went back up on deck followed by Husseini. There was obviously no point in hanging around so I went straight over the side, started the outboard and turned for home.

The current seemed stronger somehow and it took longer for me to reach the reeds or perhaps that was only my imagination. But I finally made it and bumped against the side of the *Mary Grant* again.

Sister Claire reached down to help me over the rail. 'Any sign of Turk?' I asked her.

She shook her head. 'I've been watching from the top of the wheelhouse with the field glasses, but I haven't seen a thing. What happened?'

'He offered to let Turk and me share a hundred thousand and the chance of a fresh, clean start in life.'

'And me?' she demanded.

'I'm afraid he seems to have forgotten all about you, Sister.'

She didn't like that, but by now I was getting anxious and climbed up on top of the wheelhouse to review the situation. Sister Claire clambered up beside me. The launch was still in the same position, straining at the anchor. One of the soldiers was behind the Browning machine gun, the other stood talking to Husseini at the rail.

I'll never know what went wrong, but suddenly Turk sounded right underneath them, grabbing at the bottom rung of the ladder. The most likely explanation would seem to be that he ran out of air or perhaps it was the drugs or his wound that caused the trouble.

In any event, Husseini moving with commendable speed for a third-rater who was never going to get anywhere, was down the ladder in a flash and secured a grasp on Turk's harness.

They got him out of the water and over the rail and when they finally dragged him to his feet between them he was minus his aqualung. Taleb came out on deck at that moment and joined them.

'Oh, dear God in heaven,' Sister Claire whispered.

I focussed the glasses and Turk's emaciated face jumped out at me for the last time. He was actually laughing, head thrown back when Taleb pulled out an automatic and shot him at point black range.

With a sound of thunder, the launch seemed to be blown clear out of the water. Pieces of the hull and deck were tossed hundreds of yards through the air, there was suddenly a dense pall of black smoke rolling across the water.

And then a sudden eddy of wind from the sea pushed it to one side and I saw the launch had entirely disappeared.

13

Rough Weather

I dropped to the deck and ran into the wheel-house, cursing like a madman. It was the work of a moment to start the engines and I reversed out of the reeds into the stream and spun the wheel.

There was wreckage everywhere, much of it being carried away fast by the current out in the channel. We came across one body, or to be more accurate, part of one, a soldier by the uniform, but nothing else. Sister Claire crouched over the rail, peering into the smoke which still clung to the surface of the water.

I leaned out of the window and said, 'It's no good. At the range Taleb shot him, he was probably dead before the explosion.'

She waved a hand for me to be quiet. 'One moment. I thought I heard something.'

I cut the engines and was immediately aware of a faint cry from somewhere on the port side. I started the engines again, turned the wheel and moved on through the smoke. There was wreckage all over the place.

Sister Claire called suddenly, 'Stop the engines! Stop them!'

The voice was very close now. Someone was hanging on to a hatch a few yards in front of us. For a moment, I was touched by a wild, eager hope and then, when we were close enough, I saw that it was Taleb.

I started the engines and he cried out, 'Help me! For God's sake, help me!'

There was a considerable amount of blood on his face from a scalp wound and his clothes were badly burned. I didn't feel even a hint of compassion.

Sister Claire turned to me desperately. 'For pity's sake, Mr Nelson, we must help him.'

'In a pig's eye,' I told her. 'He just murdered

the best friend I ever had. He can drown as far as I'm concerned.'

I was suddenly filled with such anger that I rushed from the wheelhouse and leaned over the rail. 'Do you hear that, you bastard?'

I could have sworn there was the ghost of a smile on his mouth, but at that moment, Sister Claire swung me round and slapped me solidly across the face as she might have slapped someone undergoing a fit of hysteria.

'You must allow me to save him!' she cried. 'You shall!'

I stared down at her, a hand to my cheek. 'You're always telling me what to do, aren't you, Sister? Well not this time. If you want to help him, go ahead, but not me. I wouldn't even pull him over the rail for you.'

I moved back to the wheelhouse without giving her a chance to reply. When I looked out, she had opened the rail and dropped the ladder. Taleb swam across to it wearily. She put out a hand to take the one he raised to her.

This time, he really was smiling and I went out of the wheelhouse on the run, reaching for the Smith and Wesson, but I was too late. As she took that outstretched hand, he brought the other up out of the water clutching the same automatic he had used to kill Turk and shot her.

She was thrown back by the violence of the blow and he dropped into the water again. As I reached the gap in the rail and levelled the Smith and Wesson, he actually laughed at me.

When I pulled the trigger there was only a hollow click and so great was my rage that I threw it at him, catching him between the eyes. He slipped beneath the surface one hand clutching at air briefly, then that, too, disappeared.

I carried her below and laid her out on her bunk. Her eyes were closed, face very white so that for a moment, I thought she was dead which didn't surprise me when I pushed up her sweater and saw that the wound was just below the left breast and there was no exit hole.

Quite suddenly her eyelids fluttered. She smiled faintly. 'How bad is it, Mr Nelson?'

'Bad enough.' What really worried me was the absence of external bleeding, but I wasn't going to tell her that. 'You need a doctor without too much delay.'

'There are doctors in Ibiza.'

'A lot quicker to try one of the Algerian coastal towns.'

'You know what that would mean.' She shook her head. 'Twelve hours to Ibiza. If you give me morphine I'll sleep for most of the trip.'

'Please, Mr Nelson.' She reached out and clutched my hand tightly. 'We have a contract or had you forgotten?' She eased back, eyes closing. 'Ten thousand dollars was the sum mentioned.'

'Still wanting your own way right to the bitter end.'

I tried to release my hand. She held on tight and the eyelids fluttered again. 'Ibiza. Promise me.'

'All right,' I said. 'You win. Now lie still while I fix you up.'

Not that there was much that I could do. I got out the medical kit and taped a sterile dressing over the wound then I gave her a morphine shot. A lot of the strain went out of her then and she looked extraordinarily peaceful so I covered her with blankets, tied a sheet round the bunk to hold her in place and went up on deck.

It was still raining hard and the *Mary Grant* had floated in against the reeds along with a considerable amount of wreckage. There was really no time to be lost now. She had said twelve hours to Ibiza. I would have to see what could be done about that.

I started the engines, moved into midstream and the current pulled us out through the estuary.

It was worse than it had been on the way in – heavy, driving rain with winds about force five or six, although this was a pure estimate on my part, for when I tried to get a weather report on the radio I found that it had been smashed by a stray bullet.

It was uncomfortable enough in the wheel-house with the rain driving in through the empty windows and I was soon soaked to the skin in spite of the yellow oilskin coat and sou'wester that I found in one of the lockers.

Under the charts was another of Turk's bottles, the usual rotgut. Cheap, Spanish brandy, but it helped with the cold and I was going to need something to get me through the hours which lay ahead. That much was obvious.

The navigation lights were still working which was something of a surprise and so were the decklights. I switched them all on as dusk fell. It made me feel less lonely.

It was a queer, mad feeling, out there alone under that darkening sky. The woman dying or close to it. Taleb lying in the mud at the bottom of the Khufra, and Turk . . . but that would not bear thinking of.

Once in Vietnam I was being decorated at an award ceremony by some General in from

313

Washington for a sight-seeing tour. After pinning the D.F.C. and the Vietnamese Cross of Valor on my manly chest, I heard him ask the Squadron Commander what I'd done. He told him I'd baled out twice at twenty thousand feet after being hit by ground-to-air missiles.

The General turned, clapped me on both arms and said, with considerable respect, 'Well, I'll say one thing for you, Nelson. You must be one hell of a survivor.'

Now, I was beginning to wonder whether the ability to survive was enough. Had ever been enough.

I must have stayed up there at least three hours the first time before putting the boat on automatic pilot and going below to see how she was.

She seemed peaceful enough in spite of the slapping of the waves against the hull. I went into the galley and made some coffee and tried to thaw out for a while, but the pounding against the hull seemed to get worse so I went back up on deck and took the wheel again.

Once, I saw the red and green navigation lights of a steamer a mile or so to starboard and for a wild moment thought of turning towards it, but the lights disappeared almost instantly in a drift of rain.

The *Mary Grant* ploughed on into the darkness. There was a really heavy swell running now, spray dashing in through the shattered windows of the wheelhouse with considerable force, but those magnificent Penta engines didn't falter for a moment.

I stuck it out manfully for another couple of hours, but by then I'd been standing so long that my leg was really hurting and the arm didn't feel too good either. I put the automatic pilot in charge again and went below.

When I went into her cabin, Sister Claire was still asleep or so it seemed. I opened the medical chest, found a morphine ampoule and gave myself a shot. When I looked up, her eyes were open and she was watching me.

'Are you in pain, Mr Nelson?'

'I'll be all right.'

'It's noisy out there.'

'There's a sea running, that's all. Nothing to worry about.'

'Poor Mr Nelson.' She closed her eyes and smiled painfully. 'I've been something of a burden since that night I came running out of the darkness by the Mill at La Grande.'

'It was no worse than being hit by a rather light truck,' I told her.

She was still smiling. 'What was it you said I was? The most bloody infuriating woman you'd ever known?'

'I was forgetting my old Aunt Hannah. You'd better get some rest now.'

She didn't reply – just lay there, eyes closed. As I started to move, she said, 'Is the statue safe?'

'As far as I know.'

I found the bundle under her bunk and unwrapped the image, holding it up for her to see. She nodded as if satisfied. 'Put it here beside me.'

Which I did and then, as I turned to the door she said quietly, 'You thought I was hard on you, you and Mr Turkovich.'

'Now and then.'

She opened her eyes and smiled. 'No, dear friend, I simply was never willing to accept less than you were truly worth.'

The eyes closed again which was as well for I hadn't a single damn thing left to say. I went up on deck to check that things were in order, then returned to the galley and made more coffee.

I sat at the table in the saloon, warming my hands on the tin cup, staring into space, thinking about what she had said, suddenly more tired than I had been in years. What a woman. What an infuriating . . .

I folded my arms and rested my head for a moment only, suddenly unable to think straight any more.

She was calling to me insistently, I was aware of that and came awake with a start to find myself ankle-deep in water. I ran into her cabin and found her trying to push herself up on one elbow.

'How long has it been like this?' I demanded.

Her voice was much stronger now. 'I'm sorry, I was sleeping. I've only just awakened. Is it bad?'

I didn't bother to reply, but went out fast, splashing through the saloon and went up the companionway. From the quality of the light I judged it to be about five a.m. which meant that I had slept for at least four hours. It was no longer raining, but we were running through sea fog so thick that visibility was reduced to a few yards.

The *Mary Grant* was rolling sluggishly, that much was self-evident and her speed was greatly reduced. I went into the wheelhouse, found a torch and went down to the engine room. There was water everywhere, just as in the saloon, welling up out of the metal hatch giving access to the scuppers.

The main pump was electric which was something. I got it going then went up on deck to see what was happening. When I looked over the side, a heavy stream of discoloured water was being forced through the outlet pipe.

I returned to the wheelhouse and consulted the chart. We had to be close to home now, but there was no way of knowing with any accuracy because of the fog and our speed had obviously suffered drastically during the past hour or two. In other circumstances, I would have kept right on going, straight into Ibiza harbour, but the way things looked now it seemed that we might be lucky to make Formentera.

The boat was moving much less sluggishly and when I took the helm, she answered reasonably well. I altered course a couple of points and went down to the engine room.

When I got the hatch off and dropped into the scuppers there was still a good two feet of water swilling about inside. I crawled forward, the flashlight between my teeth, unpleasantly aware of the stench to be found in any ship's bilge.

The trouble was plain to see when I reached the bows for there was a whole series of ragged bullet holes in the hull at this point and each time she dipped, water poured through in a series of jets.

As I started to withdraw, the *Mary Grant* lifted across a big one and plunged down again. The water level rose suddenly, passing right over my head.

I have never known such fear and yet, as I scrambled back desperately it was not myself I was thinking about, but of Sister Claire and what would befall her if anything happened to me.

The water receded into the stern as the prow lifted to the next wave and I scrambled through the hatch while the going was good. When I went back down to the saloon, there seemed to be just as much water about as before which didn't look healthy.

When I went into the cabin she was slightly on her side, face turned towards the door. 'How is it?' she said.

'Fine, nothing to worry about. A slight leak, but nothing the pumps can't handle. We'll be landing soon, I promise you.'

'I know we will, Mr Nelson. I have every

confidence in you.' She smiled calmly and lay back.

I went up on deck. The fog seemed to be lifting a little and we were still moving on, but sluggishly again. It seemed obvious that the electric pump couldn't handle the situation. There was a hand pump in the stern as I remembered. I primed it quickly, then squatted beside it, working the handle backwards and forwards viogorously with my good hand. A stream of water spilled out across the deck and over the side. Not much perhaps, but it was better than nothing.

An hour of that, was an hour too much and life became one long ache, but I didn't dare stop for the *Mary Grant* was moving more slowly than ever now.

Finally I stopped and went below. It was knee-deep in the companionway and when I went into the cabin, she was trying to sit up, pulling with one hand at the knotted sheet which held her in place.

'Time to go,' I said.

'Things are that bad?'

'There's always the inflatable with the outboard motor. We'll be all right.'

'And the gold?'

But there was only one answer to that. I took several deep breaths to give myself courage and strength and picked her up in my arms, then I waded out through the saloon and went up the companionway. I laid her down on the deck, none too gently, I'm afraid, but my wound had opened and my arm was on fire, blood soaking the sleeve.

She opened her eyes and said. 'The statue, Mr Nelson. We can save that at least.'

I went down to her cabin to get it, so tired by now that on the way back, I had the feeling at one point that I would never make it up the companionway. But I did and laid the statue down on the deck. She put her right arm about it, I straightened up wearily, ready to return to the pump and a miracle happened.

The fog rolled away as if by magic and there, no more than half a mile away, the cliffs of the south west coast of Ibiza lifted into the morning.

I slumped down on the deck beside her, laughing weakly. She said, 'What is it, Mr Nelson?'

'Ibiza,' I told her. 'We must have by-passed Formentera in the fog. We're nearly home.'

She smiled faintly. 'I never doubted that you would get me there, not for a moment, Mr Nelson. Does that surprise you?'

But I was beyond speech, crawled back to the stern and started to pump. Approximately half an hour later I took the *Mary Grant* through the channel into the bay at Tijola and ran her straight up on to the beach.

I cut the engines, came out of the wheelhouse and dropped to one knee beside her. 'Well, we made it. I'll go and get help.' Her eyes remained closed and I said in some alarm, 'Sister?'

She opened them and her smile was – how can I describe it? – radiant. 'That night on the road at La Grande. You were not there by accident, my friend. You know that now. All is for the best. Everything has a purpose.'

The eyes closed. I left her there, jumped down from the prow to the beach and started to run towards some fishermen mending nets at the other end of the beach, shouting hoarsely.

14

A Dying Fall

It was evening when they let me out of the hospital and only then because I insisted on discharging myself. Voluntarily against every argument the doctor could offer. My arm didn't hurt any more. It had simply ceased to exist like the rest of me. I survived, but only just, a slight, bright flame at the centre of nothingness.

The jeep was at the edge of the car park and as I limped towards it, a match flared, pulling Lieutenant Cordoba's melancholy face out of the darkness.

'Ah, Senor Nelson, so there you are?'

'Only just.'

He gave me a cigarette and lit it for me. The smoke caught at the back of my throat and I started to cough.

He said gravely, 'You should be in bed.'

'Or my coffin,' I said. 'It depends on your point of view. I've just lost a friend in the doctor up there.'

'I can imagine. Medical men, within my experience at least, prefer to save life.' He had been leaning against the jeep and now, he straightened. 'You are a stubborn man, but that is your own affair. You accept that in allowing you to leave this place I am not officially releasing you? There are many difficult questions you will have to answer later.'

'Fair enough.'

'Very well. You may go.' He hesitated. 'I am sorry about your friend, the good Senor Turk. More sorry than I can say.'

'So am I.'

'Are you sure you will be able to drive?'

'I don't see why not.'

I got behind the wheel and took my arm

326

out of the sling. I flexed my hand for a moment then switched on the engine.

It was a fine night with the moon rising all the way out and along the coast past the Mill at La Grande where it had all started, only this time I didn't stop.

When I reached the gates of the Villa Rose, Old Jose appeared as usual with the Alsatian snapping playfully through the bars. The old man showed no particular surprise at seeing me. Simply nodded and went back inside his hut and operated the gates.

Carlo, when he opened the front door and found me standing there, was not only astonished, but showed it. 'Senor Nelson,' he said stupidly.

'As you can see, the dead walk,' I told him. 'Is she at home?'

I didn't wait to be asked, simply brushed past him and went inside. There was no sign of Lillie in the salon and I went up the stairway and out through the French window to the terrace.

I called, 'Heh, Lillie, where are you?'

And then I saw her, down at the point on the small terrace above the bay.

I went down the marble steps on rubber legs and drifted through the garden towards her, or so it seemed. She had turned from looking out to sea and stood facing me in the most incredibly transparent dress of midnight blue, the long, dark hair flowing to the shoulders, a tall, cool glass in her left hand.

Dear Lillie, Darling Lillie. Every man's dream woman. A beautiful fantasy and I suddenly wondered if she'd ever really existed at all.

'Jack?' she said in a strange, high-pitched voice.

'As ever was, angel. Home is the sailor from the sea.'

She tossed her glass over the terrace with a quick dramatic gesture to smash on the rocks below and floated towards me until she was close enough for me to smell the rich perfume, see the shadow of the naked breasts under that fantastic dress.

'You're hurt, lover. Your arm.'

I glanced down at the sling and held her off with my good arm. 'Turk's had it, Lillie,' I said simply.

The mouth went slack. There was a strange, wild look in her eyes. 'Dead?' she said. 'Turk?'

'And Taleb – the good Colonel. He's feeding the fish too.'

Things were beginning to blur a little at the edges and I had to breathe rather deeply to stop myself from falling down.

Her voice was the merest whisper when she said, 'And Sister Claire?'

'Oh, she died in hospital about two hours ago.'

She turned away, clutching at the balustrade as if overcome. It was a good performance.

I said quietly, 'Why did you do it, Lillie? Why did you sell us out?'

And she didn't attempt to deny it, not for a moment, that was the strangest thing of all.

'How did you know?' she said dully.

'The way Taleb's boys managed to get in here so easily to grab Sister Claire that night never did make much sense to me. Not when one considers that highly expensive electronic warning system you had fitted round the walls.'

'I've been known to switch it off when I'm expecting company.'

'The right company, Lillie.' I shook my head. 'It had to be you. There was no other explanation. I saw Taleb in Zarza. He admitted to me himself that he knew we'd left, knew when to expect us. In fact, the night we were due to arrive he was waiting for us at the mouth of the Khufra. As it happens, we went in by a much more difficult back route. The one thing we hadn't mentioned in front of you, Lillie. I didn't know about it myself until Turk told me when we were closing in on the Algerian coast.'

'That doesn't prove a thing.'

'No, that's true. On the other hand you

did know we were going to be somewhere in the vicinity of Zarza which was exactly where Taleb showed. Something of a coincidence when you consider he had ten thousand square miles of the Khufra to play with.'

There was a kind of animal growl behind me. I thought it was the Alsatian, but when I turned, it was only Carl getting ready to spring.

Lillie shook her head and said quickly, 'No, leave it.'

It was a measure of her power over him that he did exactly that and she went to the drinks trolley and poured a rather large measure of gin into a fresh glass. 'All right, lover, so what? You can't prove a thing.'

'Oh, I accept that,' I said, 'but maybe that doesn't matter. Maybe the only important thing in the final analysis is that I know. How did it happen, Lillie? How did you get together?'

'He turned up here at the gate asking to see me that first night you brought her here, just after you'd left. God, but he was a cool one. Said he just wanted a chat.'

'And you listened?'

'He offered me two hundred thousand dollars if I'd help him.'

'And you fell for it?' I suppose my astonishment showed for there was something here that I didn't understand. 'Come off it, Lillie, you used to get more than that for a single movie.'

'I'm glad you used the past tense,' she said. 'If you want it straight, I'm up to my ears in debt. Anything I own in the States is in hock to the government for back taxes and that last movie I made – that Italian stinkeroo that sank without trace? I haven't seen a single dollar bill on that little item, I was only in for a percentage on profits and there haven't been any.'

'And the M.G.M. offer?'

'All they showed me was the door.' She shook her head and said calmly, 'Nobody wants me, lover. I'm through. All washed up.'

'As they say in the movies . . .'

She went very still. 'What in the hell are you getting at?'

'You, you stupid, selfish bitch,' I said. 'Do you know what's wrong with you? You've been playing a part for so long you don't know what's real any more.'

She was angry now – no, more than that – terrified. 'You shut your mouth and get out of here. Was I any worse than you and the Turk? You were really going to take that stupid kid to the cleaners between you or are you going to deny that?'

'Turk, Sister Claire, Taleb – all dead, Lillie,' I said. 'This is for real. This is happening. This time, it isn't just a re-run of one of your old movies. When the warder closes the gate on you, the cell won't go away when somebody shouts cut.'

'Carlo!' she screamed.

As he made his move I swung round and produced an automatic from inside my sling. 'Let's hold it right there.'

He crouched to spring, those great arms ready and Lieutenant Cordoba moved out of the bushes. He didn't even bother to draw his gun, just stood there, hands on hips. 'I would advise you to do as he suggests, my friend,' he called softly, then he took a whistle from his pocket and blew it.

I said to Lillie, 'He's with me, I'm afraid. Came in the back of the jeep. Didn't they handle it that way in a movie you made about fifteen years ago?'

Carlo didn't make a sound, simply launched himself at me. I was tired, but not too tired to get out of the way fast and he went straight over the balustrade in a shallow dive down to the rocks below.

It didn't have the slightest effect on Lillie or what followed when police vehicles crunched to a halt in the gravel of the drive and reinforcements arrived on the run.

She looked at me in bewilderment. 'Jack, lover? What am I going to do?'

'Oh, you'll get by,' I said. 'The Spaniards don't like to lean on women and I can just see you in black when you take the stand. They'll love you.'

'You bastard,' she said.

'A couple of years – maybe less. You'll be back in the movies before you know it because this time they'll want you, sweetheart. You'll be news again.'

She tried to get at me, fingers hooked for

my eyes, every unprintable word I'd ever heard coming straight up from the sewer.

It took Cordoba and three of his men to hold her. She was still screaming as I got into the jeep and drove away.

The little church was on the outskirts of Ibiza overlooking the sea. When I went in, it was very quiet and there was a blaze of candles down by the altar.

The coffin was on a trestle and Claire Bouvier lay inside eyes closed, hands folded on the breast. They had dressed her in the nun's habit again. She looked very peaceful.

The statue of Our Lady of Tizi Benou stood on a small table at the head of the coffin, candles flickering in front of it and half a dozen nuns of the Order of the Little Sisters of Pity kept vigil, kneeling in prayer at the altar rail.

I stood looking down at her for a while. As I say, she looked very peaceful and I was reminded of that olive grove in the sunshine when she had told me the whole story and then I remembered something else. That sentimentality was something she'd never had any time for which meant that she certainly wouldn't have approved of me standing here like this.

I turned to go and a priest came out of the vestry quietly. He walked towards the altar, paused, then came towards me. 'Mr Nelson?' He had an Irish accent. Belfast, from the sound of it.

'That's right.'

'I thought so. You were pointed out to me at the hospital.' He held out his hand. 'I am Monsignor Cathal O'Brien. They flew me in from Barcelona this morning, I'm acting for the Vatican in this matter.'

I liked him and not for any better reason than the fact that he looked as if he'd once been a useful light-heavy-weight boxer and his nose had been broken a couple of times.

He put a hand on the head of Our Lady of Tizi Benou very lightly and his face softened. 'Isn't this the most incredible thing you ever did see, Mr Nelson? A wonderful testament of faith.'

'Actually, it was made by the great Saracen silversmith, Amor Khalif, during the eleventh century,' I told him.

'And why not?' he demanded. 'The last time I commissioned a church I used a Jewish architect.' He took a hand out of his pocket. 'Here, I've got something for you. Sister Claire wanted you to have it.'

I looked down at the medal of St Martin de Porres on its silver chain. 'You mean you saw her before she died?'

'I was with her to the end. She spoke very highly of you, Mr Nelson and there's one other matter. Something she was most insistent on. It seems we owe you the sum of ten thousand dollars.'

I said slowly, 'It doesn't matter. I don't want it.'

'I'm afraid I've no choice, Mr Nelson. As I say, she was most insistent. She made me give her my solemn promise that the matter would be attended to in accordance with her wishes. I got the impression that she looked upon it as a matter of honour.'

'We had a contract,' I said.

'So I understand.' He smiled. 'Anyway, if you'll leave me your address . . .'

I went out and walked past the jeep to the low wall on the other side of the road. The moonlight glittered on the sea, a small wind ruffled my hair and I suddenly felt more alone than I'd ever done in my life before.

A matter of honour. My God, what a woman. What an infuriating, single-minded, pig-headed, wonderful woman.

One thing was certain. Everything was changed, as she had once said. Nothing would ever be the same again.

A cloud passed across the face of the moon. I was suddenly cold and my leg was beginning to hurt. Very carefully, I stowed the medal and chain away in my breast pocket, then turned and walked back to the jeep.

Dark Justice
Jack Higgins

It is night in Manhattan. The President of the United States is scheduled to have dinner with an old friend, but in the building across the street, a man has disabled the security and stands at a window, a rifle in his hand.

The assassination doesn't go according to plan, but this is only the beginning. Someone is recruiting a shadowy network of agents with the intention of creating terror.

Their range is broad, their identities masked, their methods subtle. White House operative Blake Johnson and his opposite number in British intelligence, Sean Dillon, set out to trace the source of the havoc, but behind the first man lies another, and behind him another still. And that man is not pleased by the interference. Soon, he will target them all: Johnson, Dillon, Dillon's colleagues. And one of them will fall....

'Open a Jack Higgins novel and you'll encounter a master craftsman at the peak of his powers . . . first-rate tales of intrigue, suspense and full-on action'   *Sunday Express*

0-00-712723-5

Without Mercy

Jack Higgins

In Jack Higgins' acclaimed bestseller *Dark Justice*, intelligence operative Sean Dillon and his colleagues in Britain and the United States beat back a terrible enemy, but at an equally terrible cost. One of them was shot, another run down in the street. Both were expected to survive – but only one of them does.

As Detective Superintendent Hannah Bernstein of Special Branch lies recuperating in the hospital, a dark shadow from their past, scarred deep by hatred, steals across the room and finishes the job. Consumed by grief and rage, Dillon, Blake, Ferguson and all who loved Hannah swear vengeance, no matter where it takes them. But they have no idea of the searing journey upon which they are about to embark – nor of the war which will change them all.

'Higgins is a master of his craft'   *Daily Telegraph*

ISBN 978-0-00-719945-7

What's next?

Tell us the name of an author you love

Jack Higgins   Go ▶

and we'll find your next great book.